W9-BVG-637

*She whipped out a bale of "C" notes from her outrageous cleavage and tossed it onto the bar top. You could have heard two cockroaches fornicating on Mars in the sledgehammer silence.*

*I leaned into Streak's ear and whispered, "Jesus Christ, get yourself together. Let's split. Two Outfit Aces are out to hit you!"*

*Streak's face turned ashen.*

*Some joker expressing the collective passion of the clientele shouted, "Girl, I oughta stick you up."*

*Streak glanced around anxiously and drew a Magnum pistol. He scooped up the bundle into his overcoat pocket. We threaded our way back to the street. The three of us got into a cab.*

*Streak checked into a fleabag hotel on the Westside. His fox went into the shower. He slumped down on the side of the bed. I sat down beside him.*

*He moaned, "Slim, it's the end of the world."*

*I said, "Get in the wind, Streak. It's a big world."*

Middleton Public Library
7425 Hubbard Ave
Middleton, WI 53562

## Other Titles by Iceberg Slim

Middleton Public Library
7425 Hubbard Ave
Middleton, WI 53562

# Airtight Willie & Me

## The Story of the South's Black Underworld

# ICEBERG SLIM

CASH MONEY CONTENT

# Airtight Willie & Me

Copyright © 2013 by Robert Beck Estate

Cash Money Content™ and all associated logos are trademarks of
Cash Money Content LLC.

All Rights Reserved. No part of this book may be used or reproduced in
any manner whatsoever without written permission of the publisher,
except where permitted by law.

Any similarity to persons living or dead is purely coincidental.

First Trade Paperback Edition: March 2013

Book Layout: Peng Olaguera/ISPN

Cover Design: MJCDesign

For further information log onto www.CashMoneyContent.com

Library of Congress Control Number: 22011931201

ISBN: 978-1-936399-15-4 pbk

ISBN: 978-1-936399-16-1 ebook

10 9 8 7 6 5 4 3 2

Printed in the United States

*This volume is dedicated to time.*
*It gives us memories, fine wine, and wrinkles.*
*But the only thing worse than getting old is not getting old.*
*So here's to time, dear reader, yours and mine.*
*May you have many more wrinkles, a lot of fine wine,*
*and memories to last two lifetimes.*

# Airtight Willie & Me

# AIRTIGHT WILLIE & ME

**B**ack in the days when bad girls humped good bread into my pockets, con man, Airtight Willie and pimp . . . me . . . lay in a double bunk cell on a tier in Chicago Cook's County Jail. I was having one bitch kitty of a time tuning out the interracial sewer-mouth shucking and jiving and playing the "dozens" from cell to cell on our tier.

"Lee, your mama is a freakish bitch that hasta crap in a ditch 'cause she humped a railroad switch."

"Hal, your raw-ass mammy had bad luck. That drunk bitch got platoon-raped in an army truck."

Airtight Willie leapt off his bunk screeching and made it a "dozens" roundelay. "Dummy up, you square-ass punks. Both you muthafuckahs got mamas so loose and wide they gotta play the zoo to cop elephant woo."

I was winding up a stone and a day. I would hit those cold-blooded streets four brights (mornings); hence, whoreless! I mean, I was desperately trying (in the flare of matches they lit across the courtyard) to monitor the shuck and jive of the whores and jaspers (pimpese for lesbians) as they ate each other out and banged their pygmy cocks together.

I figured by culling the bullshit coming from across the way, I might pick up a dropped name and a line on at least one three-way money tree. Maybe she'd be winding up a bit. Maybe some joker had blown one. Maybe I could fly one a couple of my magnetized copping kites (high-voltage letters) when I hit the bricks and steal a HO!

Slippery Airtight Willie, on the bunk above me, had slid into mind reading sure as he was rotten.

I saw his mongoose face peek down at me as he said in his molasses drawl, "Slim, I ain't complimented nobody no time before. But I gotta say you ain't nothing but a foxy dude to stop playing for skunk bitches like them over there and deciding to play the con with me in them streets."

I said sleepily, "Yeah, Willie . . . A ho ain't worth a thimble of poo-poo."

Willie, needing a partner to play the con, had given me a six-weeks crash course in how to stop and qualify (any money to play for? . . . ever been flimflammed before?) a mark, put him on the send (he goes to get his money), and how to rip him off with cross-fire dialogue between us.

I sure needed to play Willie's game. At least until I got the bread to lay down on a far-out ride (maybe a vintage Rolls, fur trimmed), B.R. (flash cash), and threads to dazzle and lure whores to within stealing or "turn-out" copping range.

A match flared in a cell across the way illuminating two broads sixty-nining while a third broad, wearing a crude dildo fashioned from a toilet brush, humped dog-fashion behind one.

An excited chump, on the tier above us, apparently was baring his stiff problem to the trio. He screamed through the open windows into the unusually warm January night. "You long-cunt bitches, gander this big, black pretty I'm holding and eat your freakish hearts out!"

A shrill-voiced broad lopped off his fake balls. "Dave Jones, this is Cora Brown. You old snaggletoothed fag. You know I know that thing you flashing wasn't nothing in them streets but a handle for dudes to flip you over with."

I thought about some of the harrowing disadvantages in playing con. A felony bust if caught. A morgue slab if a cutthroat mark woke up before he was "blowed off." And most unpleasant of all was the epidemic scuttlebutt that grifters often got bone tired and foot sore searching for a qualifiable mark.

Willie validated his moniker and soft shoed onto my wavelength again. He crooned, "Slim, I got a lot of confidence in you. I'm gonna angle my ass off as soon as I get in the wind this morning scoring for transportation and other nit shit we gonna need. Howzit sound, pal-of-mine?"

I barely heard him because I was trying to pluck out from the din across the way a line on a café-au-lait fox. She was fingering into the crimson slash in her jet brush to drool the voyeur chumps upstairs. She was boasting how she'd cut her old man loose during visiting hours that very day.

I said, "It sounds sweet, Willie . . . And sweeter is when we start taking off those big stings! . . ."

As I fell asleep, I heard young joker hollering he was a helluva pimp.

The ball-lopper across the way shrilled, "Joe Thomas, bullshit everybody but Cora Brown. I heard you ate everything except the nails in Little Bit's shoes all night last summer. At the time, she told me, she was holding enough bread to burn up a herd of wet cattle. She gave you a buck for grits and greens. No playing, chump! Dummy up!"

The icy morning of my release, my teeth chattered in the sleazy thin benny belonging to some slight-of-hand bastard in property. He had switched me out of my stable-trimmed, leather-whore catcher. I was a hundred yards down California Avenue when the sudden blast of a horn behind me almost tinkled me. I got in the snow-dappled heap. Willie grinned and passed me a half-full, half-pint of gin.

He said, "Kill it." Then he looked me up and down. A moment later, he said, "We gotta go and score for decent bennys and bread to make up a playing boodle."

He briefed me how on the way to a medium-size department store on State Street. We went in through different entrances. I dug Willie in position to score. My arm swept perfume bottles off a counter with a great clatter as I collapsed to the stone floor. I performed an attention-grabbing, flop-tongued epileptic seizure that sucked men's wear empty of personnel.

Some compassionate soul rammed a metal glasses case into my mouth. I peeked through the forest of legs at Willie. He had liberated two bennys off hangers and was nonchalantly till tapping (rifling a cash register) men's-wear bread. He blurred through a side door. I recovered, mouthing baroque gratitude. I walked my eyes heavenward. I profusely thanked J.C. and the mob surrounding me (as per Willie's instructions) as I oozed away to the sidewalk.

Our bennys were good fits. But the scratch from the till was too thin to make up a viable boodle. On Clark Street, Willie pulled to the curb and leaped from the car. I got under the wheel.

Willie walked, with head down, toward a florid fatso in ritzy togs, coming down the sidewalk, bent against the hooligan wind. Two feet from the target, Willie spat a gob of spit into the wind and fouled the front of the dude's impeccable benny. I watched Willie rush to him, with jaws flapping apology. He feverishly wiped the dude clean of spittle—and his billfold from the well (inside breast pocket).

As I was driving toward the Southside, Willie stopped arranging a wad of play money to say, "We got five hundred frog skins to make up boodle that will give the suckers blues with a toothache . . . Say, we better blow some of the pressure in our balls into some jazzy fox to loosen up for the marks."

I said, "Man, I don't dig no bought snatch, and I'm too noble to beg for it."

He busted out laughing. "Slim, I'm gonna hip you how to bang the choicest pros with no pay, no bed!"

We parked a half hour while he ran down his poontang swindle. In the Seventies on Cottage Grove Avenue, he told me to pull over and park in front of the Moon Glo Bar. I did, and dug on the vision he had dug. He caressed his tinted fly.

She hustled her Pet-of-the-Year type curves toward us. Her face was copper satin, pure electric, like those ball-blasting Aztec broads on the calendars printed in Spanish.

He opened the car door and said hoarsely, "Ain't no way we can do better than her. Don't forget the cues we rehearsed, and remember, you're stone-deaf and dumb. You're a champ chump from the Big Foot Country (Deep South), and you're creaming to get laid."

I enjoyed an interior smirk. Remember? A few con items? Willie, the rectum, was apparently unhip I had memorized an arsenal of howitzer motivators I'd kept on instant alert inside my skull. I'd barraged them daily for three years to persuade a ten ho stable to hump my pockets obese.

Willie suddenly hammered his fist down on my hat crown. I glanced into the rearview mirror. My lid was telescoped into a porkpie, cocked stupidly on the side of my long head.

He said, "Now you look the part, pardner."

He sprang to the sidewalk, whipping off his hat. His face was booby-trapped with pearly con as he rapped his opener. She darted a glance in my direction. He had cracked comedic shit on her to set me up as flim-flamee and her as fuckee. She giggled her epic ass off.

She scooted across the seat close to me as Willie boxed her in and shut the car door. I yo-yoed my Adams Apple as I imagined a mute bumpkin would, if pressed against her pulse-sprinting heat.

Willie said, "Sharlene Hill, this is Amos . . . Did you say yur last name was Johnson, buddy?"

I nodded and wiped my brow with the back of my hand.

She giggled and said, "Hi, Bootie, Cootie."

Willie leaned across her and said, "She boss cute enough for that hundred dollars you want to spend?"

Slack jawed, I nodded vigorously. Then I frowned and got pencil and pad, rubber banded to the sun visor. She watched me laboriously scribble, "You go first" and pass the message to Willie.

He chuckled and said, "Amos, we don't have to do it that way. I've known Sharlene since she was a baby. I'm ready to take the oath before the Supreme Court, she ain't got no bad disease like they told you down home most all the fast ladies up here is suppose to have."

I put my handkerchief across my mouth and turned my head away to cough so he could wink at her and say, "Course, if you just gotta test my confidence in her cleanness, you have to give her two hundred in advance."

I swept my eyes hungrily over her awesome thighs, exposed by the hiked-up pink suede miniskirt. I nodded furiously. She took my hand and glued it against her throbbing vulva as she rolled her belly.

Willie said, "You gonna pay her from the money in your shoe, or should I pay her from this money I'm safekeeping for you?"

I pointed toward him. He reached into his overcoat pocket and removed a blue bandana-wrapped wad holding five hundred in fifties, tens, and a hundred-dollar bill. She stopped her belly motor. She freed my hand and watched him untie the knots and count out two hundred.

It was my cue to get a severe fit of coughing and spitting. I turned away and stuck my head out the window.

Willie tied up all the cash again before her eyes. Then he leaned toward her ear, blocking sight of the money for a mini-instant. The index and middle fingers of his right hand shoved the cash down the left sleeve of his overcoat. With magician speed he simultaneously grabbed and palmed the bandana with play money, stashed in the same sleeve.

He pressed the dummy into her hands as he whispered, "Beautiful, let's rip this chump off. Put this whole grand in your bosom right next to your boss lollipops. Meet me right there in the Moon Glo in ten minutes after we cut you loose . . . for the split."

Her green neons were sparkling excitement when I took my head out of the window. Willie was airtight all right. He wouldn't even spring for the motel fin to rip her with some kind of class.

I drove around the desolate southern perimeter of the city while Willie mule-dicked her and blew off his jail cherry with the exclamation, "Oheeeeee! Slim! I'm gonna nominate her box for the hall of fame!"

But there was something about the cloying stink of their juice stew and the sloppy, kissy sound his slab meat made withdrawing that turned me off.

He climbed over the seat and said, "Pull over and let me take the wheel."

I started to pass her up. But the expression on Willie's face was pulling my coat she'd wake up if I didn't do a number with her. While Willie drove us around, I opted for her far-out skull extravaganza.

We let her go in front of the Moon Glo. She went in the front door. We cruised around the block and caught a glimpse of her cannon assing it down the alley in the back of the bar. Her pimp was going to foam at the jib when she checked in that load of play money.

The banks and postal savings offices would soon be closing, so we dirtied plates and copped pads. Next morning, at ten, we were working both sides of Garfield Boulevard on the Southside. Both of us had struck out several times at the qualifying stage with marks we had stopped.

At two thirty, Willie stopped a powerfully built older guy. I watched Willie's two grand choppers flashing as he pitched the "cut in" and "sound out" con to qualify the mark.

I had memorized both ends of our game's dialogue so I knew Willie was saying, "Forgive me, sir. My mama taught me, in her lap, it's bad manners and not Christian to disrespect a stranger's privacy. But I'm upset! I'm in need of advice from some intelligent and wise-looking colored gentleman like yourself."

I saw the mark move, with Willie, from the middle of the sidewalk to stand near the curb to hear Willie's problem. "I just got here from Mississippi. I'm carrying a lot of money from the sale of my farm. I'm confused and afraid because a friendly white man on the train from Vicksburg warned me about flimflambers . . . or something. Worse, the white man told me that banks up here give white folks five percent interest on savings and only three percent to colored people. Please, tell me, kind sir, what are flim-flappers? And does your experience with these banks make that white man tell me a lie or the truth?"

Shortly, Willie stroked an index finger across his left cheek. My cue to drop and pick up the wallet, fat with the boodle, near any big, expensive car parked on the street.

Willie touched the mark's sleeve and dipped his head toward me. At this point, Willie would be saying, "Ain't it a pity that colored man over there is so honest he's paralyzed with guilt and fear. He was lucky enough to pick up a wallet a rich-looking white man lost when he got out of that new Lincoln. I think we oughtta put his mind at ease."

Willie and the mark waved me to them. Up close, the mark's face and vibes jangled an alarm bell inside my skull.

I shakily said, "You gentlemen won't call the law, will you?"

Willie said, "We will not! Finding a wallet belonging to a rich white man sure don't make a colored man a thief in our book. The Lord has gave you a lucky day. Ain't that the truth, Mr. Ellis?"

The mark stared luminous gray eyes at me and nodded. Could he be the vengeance-hungry father of some long-ago doll I'd "turned out" and he was trying to place me?

I glanced around us suspiciously, and with a sigh of relief, I said to Willie, "Mr. Ell—"

Willie cut me off and said, "I'm Mr. Jackson."

I said, "Joe Franklin is pleased to make both your acquaintances. I'm happy, happy, two colored gentlemen with mother-wit saw me instead of two mean white folks. I been knowing all my life, good advice comes from good people, and should be rewarded—"

Willie cut in. "Hold on there, Franklin! We didn't advise you to share in your good luck . . . did we, Mr. Ellis?"

The mark's heavy blue lips pulled back in a twisted little smile. Disgust at Willie's remark wrinkled his ebonic brow. In a high-pitched voice, eerily issuing from his six-six, two-hundred-fifty pound frame, he squealed, "We surely didn't—"

I said, "Hush up, Mr. Ellis! I won't let you talk me out of it. Friends, we gonna share equally fifteen bucks or fifteen thousand bucks." I gave them a flash of apparent long green stuff inside the bulgy hide.

Willie said, "You've hit the jackpot! Let's move! The white man is positively gonna miss that load of cash!"

We steered the mark to a bench on the strip of grass that ran down the center of the boulevard. I started to examine the wallet's contents. I let excitement make me drop it. Willie scooped it up and turned away from the mark's ravenous eyes.

I started at the mark's flat, brutish profile. I recognized him! . . . from somewhere long ago!

The big vein on the mark's neck ballooned when he saw Willie let fall and retrieve our lone "C" note before he handed the wallet back to me. Willie exclaimed, "This damn thing is packed with hundred dollar bills!"

Willie gave me an evil eye because I was a split-instant tardy delivering the next line. My mind was at the brink of recalling the where-and-when about the mark.

I said, "That white man is a big-time something."

Willie said, "He could be a crooked high roller."

I said, "Maybe the money is stolen, or even counterfeit . . . What we gonna do?"

Willie said, "The money's real, but we need the help of some big-shot colored man or understanding white one. Now about you, Mr. Ellis, you know some big shot we can trust?"

Before the mark answered, I snapped my fingers and said, "I got somebody! My boss, Mr. Gilbranski. We can trust him because he loves colored folks for sure. He's been married to one for twenty years. He's got a fine suite of offices two blocks around the corner in the Milford Building. My stars, I just remember I was on an errand for Mr. Gilbranski when we had our good luck. You good people wait right here. My boss will solve our problem so we can split safe and fair."

After I left, Willie would say, "Mr. Ellis, I think we've found a pure-in-heart man and a small fortune. If he's not pure and doesn't show back here, we can't lose what we never had."

I drank greasy spoon coffee for fifteen minutes before I came back to the mark's wide grin. The mark's relaxed face jibbled a bit of the puzzle into place! OHIO! DEATH!

I pumped their hands and said, "Good people, I knew my boss is a sweetheart! The wallet belonged to a racist politician he despises. He's ready to give us equal shares of the eighteen thousand in small bills."

I paused and chuckled. "So, he couldn't have no reason whatsoever not to help us, I fibbed and told him two kinfolks was in on my good luck. He knows I've only got two kin in the world, my Uncle Otis and Aunt Lula, both he's never seen . . . He ain't gonna hassle us. He just wants to meet you and find out you're people with mother-wit and won't go crazy with the money and get him in a squeeze for coming to our rescue."

Then I said, "He's awaiting on the ninth floor of the Milford Building."

Willie touched the mark's arm, and they started to walk away.

I said loudly, "What you gentlemen gonna do, make me out a liar and fix it so my boss won't help us? I told you he knows all the kin I got is Uncle Otis and Aunt Lula. Mr. Ellis ain't no woman."

Willie shook the mark's hand and said, "Mr. Ellis, rest easy! The same arrangements I make for me, I'll make for you!"

I said, "Don't you think you oughtta tell the boss the excitement is got old Aunt Lula feeling poorly, so she went home to rest?"

While Willie was gone, I brought the mythical office and boss to life for the mark with detailed descriptions. Willie returned breathlessly, reinforcing my wonderful boss and his luxurious office.

Willie said, "Mr. Gilbranski liked me, and loves you! He was sold on my levelheadedness when I was able to put up the four thousand dollars from the sale of my farm as proof I'm used to big money. He's satisfied I wouldn't cause him no scandal. He told me he'd trust you with his life. He said to tell you, he takes care of business inside the office and you take care of me and Aunt Lula . . . I mean Mr. Ellis, outside the office."

I left to bring back Willie's and the mark's shares. At least, the mark was expecting his. When I got back, I gave Willie a manila envelope, fat with greenbacks rolled around the boodle of play money.

Willie frowned and said with great annoyance, "Where the hell is Mr. Ellis's share?"

I shrugged and said, "Mr. Gilbranski said every tub must sit on its own foundation and make its own strong bond good faith. Aunt Lula . . . I mean Mr. Ellis ain't showed his good faith in the right way."

Willie said huffily, "Since Mr. Ellis's share ain't here, take it all back! It ain't right to have mine, and he don't have his."

I said, "I didn't say Mr. Ellis couldn't get his share. All he's got to do is satisfy the boss he's a solid citizen like you did."

The mark's eyes were spewing gray fire as he flung back his overcoat to reveal what could only be the handle of a hand ax protruding from his benny's inside pocket.

He blurted out, "Mr. Jackson sure spoke the truth. I've already decided none of us is getting a share unless I get mine . . . I'll be back in two minutes, so stay here on the bench!"

Willie and I looked at each other. At this most delicate juncture, Willie was supposed to go with the mark to get his cash bond.

As we watched the mark unlock the trunk of a new Buick across the street, I said, "Willie, we oughtta cut this one loose!"

Willie said, "Shit, I got a feeling he's gonna be sweet as bee pussy. I'd play for the motherfucking devil today!"

I feverishly tried to tie the mark to some celebrated ax murder in Ohio long ago. The mark returned and counted out a stack of "C" notes. As I was stuffing the entire three grand score into my overcoat pocket, the mark vised my shoulders and balefully stared into my eyes.

He said, "Please! Mr. Franklin, don't take my money to that peckerwood if you ain't damn sure he's on the dead level!"

I said, "He's famous for shooting straight in business and everywhere."

He released me and giggled, "So am I famous . . . for shooting straight!"

I felt a bowel-gasket about to pop. As I turned away on Jell-O legs, I suddenly remembered all of the mark's grisly infamy. He'd been a construction worker, who, around twelve years before, had riddled two men at a poker table for cheating.

For a week, the Cleveland police put his mug shots in all the newspapers and cautions on all radio stations. A hundred police trapped him in a tenement. He critically wounded two detectives before his capture and was committed as hopelessly insane to a state hospital. Now, escaped or released, he would be waiting for me!

I drank another cup of greasy spoon coffee before I started back to blow him off (get free of him). I stopped and waved two hundred yards away so Willie could point me out to the mark. They looked at me. Willie stabbed his index finger toward his chest. I waggled my head "no." Willie stabbed his finger toward the mark. I waggled "yes."

I was drenched and stinking of fear sweat as the mark's long legs pumped toward me in great athletic strides. When he was midway, I saw Willie fading away fast behind the mark. Just before I ducked around the corner, the mark glanced back at Willie. He howled piercingly and streaked toward me with the grace and speed of a gazelle.

I pistoned south on Indiana Avenue. Before I turned at Fifty-sixth, to double back to our jalopy parked under the Garfield Boulevard El, I glanced back. The joker had been ultra-positively a second Jessie Owens in his youth. He was so close, I could see the gleam of his bared choppers and the glitter of the hatchet.

I couldn't have run another foot when I fell through the jalopy's open door and collapsed beside Willie at the wheel. Willie's face was pocked with sweat as he ground the starter furiously. We stared at the mark growing to the size of King Kong and heard his number thirteens grenading against the sidewalk. I got the window up just as he reached us.

I said, "Oh, Mama!" over and over at the awful sound of the hatchet as he ran around the car smashing glass. His frothy mouth was quivering with madness as he chopped a confetti of glass into the car. He was reaching through the shattered window to unlock the door when the starter caught and Willie bombed the heap away.

At that instant I made an obvious vow that I've kept to this moment!

We got a pint of tranquilizer on the far Westside and sloshed the first hits down our chins.

Willie suddenly laid out a bandana on the seat between us. He pulled out his boodle-wallet, slipped out of his overcoat, and said, "Pal-of-mine, we oughtta separate the boodle from the thirty-five-hundred frog skins so we can split right down the middle."

I stiffened at the thought he might try to switch me out of my end in the murk of fallen dusk. I placed all I held on the seat. And I was determined to challenge any suspect moves he made with the money before I had my end safely in hand.

With his overcoat off, I wasn't really worried that he was slick enough to burn me in his sweater sleeves. He shook his head as he looked at the score. He straightened out the bills. Then he made a flat package of the money. He tied it up in the wide bandana.

He glanced at a passing police car and said, "Shit, Slim, we could get busted counting the score. Here, shove it under your seat until after we cop some ribs and a motel room for the split."

I x-rayed his hands as he passed the bandana, then I pushed it under the seat. He pulled away and parked behind a rib-and-burger joint on Lake Street.

He sat there for a long time before he said, "Slim, you gonna cop the pecks?"

I was racked with closet laughter. Did he believe I was sucker enough to leave him tending the score? I said, "Cop for yourself, Willie . . . I ain't hungry."

He said, "I ain't got a 'sou' to cop with," and leaned down and pulled out the bandana.

He untied it on the seat and removed a ten-dollar bill. He put our score back under the seat, and his mitt was clean coming out, except for the sawbuck.

I hawk-eyed him as he got out and shut the door. He shivered elaborately and opened the car door. He leaned into the car and reached for his beanie draped across the back of the front seat. For only a mini-instant was his overcoat a curtain blocking him from view as he lifted off the seat.

I thought, Houdini, with four-foot arms, couldn't have plucked that score from beneath my seat at that range. Anyway, I bent over and probed until my fingertips touched it. He slammed the door shut. I felt a twinge of guilt, watching the wind flap his overcoat tails, that he was trusting me with the score.

In a couple of minutes, I heard the thunder of the Lake Street El Train pulling into the station down the street. I looked up at it passing on the way to the Loop. Was that Willie wrapped in his blue plaid benny grinning down at me from a window in the last car?

I tore open the bandana! It was a dummy loaded with

funny-money. I dug beneath the seat like a pooch for a buried bone. Nothing! I raced around the car and pawed beneath the driver's seat. Something sharp gouged blood from my thumb tip. It was a fishhook tied to a length of twine that was tied to an anchor post beneath the seat.

The cunning sonovabitch had probably choreographed the rip-off while we were in the cell. With vivid hindsight, I knew why he pretended he needed the sawbuck from the bandana. He wanted to get the fishhook into it when he put it back. Then he could reel it in with his left hand when he leaned into the car for his benny. The dummy bandana was preplanted to "blow me off" smoothly just in case I got suspicious, as I did, before he hit the wind.

I leapt behind the wheel. Maybe I could catch him in the Loop, or at one of the El stops along the way. The gas gauge was on "E," and I didn't have a cent.

I got out and inhaled deeply. I felt my belly jitterbug in the greasy clouds of soul-food aroma floating from the rib joint. I straightened my tie in a gum machine's fractured mirror, then I psyched up the mirrored mack-man staring back. "You a bad, sugar-rapping ho-stealing motherfucker . . . ain't you? Ain't nothing can stop a ho stalking stepped like you . . . Ain't that right?" Frantically I nodded yes and turned away.

I was lucky! It was black ghetto Christmas. Saturday Night! Easy to cop a ho! I'd guerilla my Watusi ass into a chrome-and-leather ho den and gattle-gun my pimp-dream shit into some mud-kicker's frosty car.

I pimp-pranced toward a ho jungle of neon blossoms a half mile away. Some ass-kicker was a cinch to be a ho short when the joints folded in the A.M.

# TO STEAL A SUPERFOX

It was late summer back in the nineteen forties. The weeks before, I had graduated from a federal prison. I was stalking ho runs in an Ohio burg. It was my birthday. I was ho-less, without a sou in my raise. I was decked out in a gold silk vine and accessories an old pal junkie ho had boosted the day before in Chicago.

Around twilight I stopped by Pretty Phil's, a pimp pal's juke saloon and two-story trick hotel. We embraced. He wiggled his lips against my ear lobe as we disengaged. I thought about the rumors that he now dug stud tours of his sphincter cave.

I cracked it was my birthday. He got on the phone and ordered a monster cake and several cases of Mums.

We sat down and snorted white lady until two A.M. and gazed through the Venetian blinds of his front window. A cavalcade of tricks, flat-backers, stuff players, and thieves paraded past. I shifted uneasily when I caught Phil's assassin Harlequin Great Dane eyeballing me enigmatically. Phil stroked her muzzle. She sighed and nested her head in his lap.

Phil gave me a rundown on every qualified, stealable ho that passed. His rundowns were boss. Sure, I appreciated the crystal blow and his plans to celebrate my birthday. But had he forgotten what a blue-ribbon pal I had been back in Cleveland several years before? He had blown into town with no ho. And worse, no wheels and frozen fireworks exploding off his dukes, necessary to cop a star ho.

I had loaned him my total flash. He had gone on to pimp a zillion. I had too much player pride to smooch his rear end to nudge his sense of all-out reciprocity. I seriously mulled the odds that Phil would test out as a chicken poo-poo amnesiac.

I stared thoughtfully at Phil's yellow bitch face. Like my scarlet doubt was a tennis ball, Phil bombed back the serve when he cracked, "Slim, honey, you hip, I know, that you got my personal pad upstairs and the use of my new wheels and ice to catch you a ho. And, pally, since you my size, play your ass off in any and all of them sixty ho catchers hanging in my closet."

He dropped a key into my shirt pocket, then he picked up a phone and called upstairs to have the linen changed. I would've kissed the gaudy mother if I hadn't been leery of inviting his tongue up my jib. Phil eased out a portly bankroll. He peeled off several "C" notes and scooted them across the tabletop.

I slid them into my shirt pocket. I was about to tell him what a thoroughbred, stand-up nigger he was when an ebonic money-magnet seized my eyes and struck me mute. She crossed the street and stood on ho point. You know, big exquisite props wide spread. Her crotch humped out to bulge her obese sex nest against her gauzy red dress. Her luminescent skin shone like indigo velour in the neon razzle. She was certified to be a bantam bundle of voluptuous headache for suckers.

Oh, I knew at first gander she was a cold-blooded magician. I saw it in her arrogant body lingo. I saw it in the wizard choreography of her long, tapered fingers. It was confirmed by her fierce killer falcon eyes.

I said dreamily, "Phil, I gotta own that slave . . . gimme a rundown on her and her master."

Phil curled his lupine lips. He gave me a look like I was that dingbat humpback of Notre Dame. He sneered, "Easy, Massa, since you gotta dream, go to Shitcon City. You could faster and more safely steal Betty Grable, Hedy Lamarr . . . every top mack man from coast to coast has a hard-on to cop that package over there. Her old man's a stone gorilla. He's shot and stomped a half-dozen niggers about that ho. She's got his nose open wide enough to shove in a coffin. Catch on, pally? She's Black Sue. She can pick a chump clean from all pockets and stashes in thirty seconds. Pally, that bitch is a Superfox Hall-of-Famer ho . . . Now gander the sweetness of the ho's style on that paddy cutting in to her."

We watched a brawny white joker in a new Buick honk desperately at the instant that he spotted the pygmy ball lyncher. I've seen excited suckers in my time, but that lame has remained without peer in my memory. He just let his chariot drive itself. He coasted through a near-collision cacophony of honking horns as he stretched his neck back and ogled her with phosphorescent eyes.

She flashed her teeth like a rabid panther. She undulated her flat gut to hook him for the killing floor. She jerked her head toward the yawning vestibule of a condemned fleabag hotel behind her. The sucker was so hot to sock it to her, he couldn't risk parking or going around the block. His wheels screeched like a cat in an Osterizer when he U-turned. He parked crookedly in front of Phil's sucker trap. He leapt out and galloped through graveyard traffic to her side of the stem.

We had seen a gleaming gold watch on his wrist. A dime-sized jeweled stickpin had been shooting pastel fire from his necktie. She stood smiling at him behind the cobwebby glass of the vestibule. Almost immediately we saw their silhouettes merge. It was like they were dancing to the seductive beat of a Top Ten hit parade tune.

Phil said, "Count the seconds, pally. That voodoo bitch is pure magic."

I started counting in my head. I had counted fifty-five seconds when the mark stepped out. He patted his hip pocket as he bullet-assed it down the sidewalk. He went into a hotel at the end of the block. His watch and stickpin were playing hooky. Black Sue peeped out and oozed down the alley across the way.

Phil said, "That Houdini bitch took them extra seconds to lift his jewelry . . . Ain't she a motherfucker? She's sent that mark to check in for fun and games. He ain't got the five bucks for the room. He's gonna piss in his pants when he finds the ho has cleaned him out and put his wallet back . . . and rebuttoned his pocket!"

I said, "That ho is two-and-a-half tons of sweet bread . . . Phil, I gotta steal that fox. I ain't never gonna be satisfied if I cop a thousand girls. Phil, I deserve that ho, and the ho deserves me. I'm gonna toss the craps for her! Back me up, old buddy!"

Phil shrugged. "Any and everything, pally. But like I laid it out front, you ain't got nothing but sucker odds. So if you want to buck the saw and get in the pit with her gorilla . . . He don't allow the ho to even rap with nothing but suckers . . . and don't forget he lugged her from New Orleans. Them pimps and hoes off'a Rampart Street got their own understanding of one another's crazy shit and savvy of their thing together. One more time, Slim, let the ho be! Darling, I don't want to cry like a cunt at your funeral."

Then Phil sighed. "Good luck, pally . . . Promise to bury you in a blue silk vine with a three-day wake."

We watched the stricken sucker stumble out to the sidewalk. He streaked back to the vestibule killing floor, where he kicked out the door glass panels. He scooted up and down the block, peeping into every joint and cranny. He was cavorting and hurting like his balls had been blow-torched. Finally, he sad-sacked into his Buick. He stomped the horses and blasted off to shake down the ghetto catacombs.

Phil's main ho, dwarfish Bitsy Red, and several hoes of his stable came in to set up the joint for the after-hours action and my birthday party. You know, stringing bunting and glitter crap around the mirrored joint.

I said, "Phil, how long has that ho been down in this burg?"

He said, "A week or so . . . Why?"

I said, "A ho with her voltage is about due to hit the wind any time . . . You know, with the heat and all . . . I better get in the streets now to make some kinda contact with the ho. How about laying some more fast rundown on me . . . like has her old man got any chump shortcomings. . . craps, hard shit, or what not?"

Phil grinned. "Like every nigger mack fresh outta big-foot country, he's sizzling for young white ho pussy . . . He's sported his dick twice at Aunt Lula's joint out at the lip of town . . . He's a half a 'C' note trick . . . cons himself he can steal one with his jib and dick. You ain't got to hit the stem to take your shot at that ho . . . Every pimp and ho in town will ease in here before daybreak. Please, pally! . . . Be cool and don't make Jabbo Ross, that's the gorilla's moniker, waste you in here and sour my roller fix for my joint."

I said, "I'll be cool, brother . . . Does Bitsy know the ho?"

Phil's Persian cat eyes ballooned with righteous indignation. Bubbles, the Dane, jerked her two hundred pounds to an ominous crouch.

Phil's contralto rap box quavered. "Slim, darling, you my main man, and I love ya. Ain't no doubt you hip. I'd cut off my right wing and my swipe for you. But I ain't gonna let you throw my bottom ho, Bitsy, in no cross with that crazy nigger Jabbo and that girl. Nigger, you got a chump yen for the morgue! You ain't taking Bitsy on that trip!"

I leaned to pat his shoulder. Bubbles issued a doomsday snarl. Phil whispered harshly, "Ho, everything is cool. Lay your bad ass down somewhere."

Bubbles sighed. She crashed down behind his chair and stared at me with malevolent eyes.

I said, "Baby, you read me wrong. I don't want Bitsy to cut into the ho with no messenger cupid bit. Maybe Bitsy is got some inside info on the ho. You know, personal scam that only a ho would be hip to."

Phil turned toward the bar and snapped his fingers. Bitsy looked up from dumping silver into the cash register. Phil's head waggled her to our table. She sat down. I had met her in Cleveland. She smiled.

Phil said, "Give my homeboy a rundown on Black Sue."

Bitsy said in a squeaky voice, "We did a lot of rapping 'fore Ross cut us loose . . . She's twenty-two or -three . . . I think. Got a crumb crusher, a daughter, in a state foster home back in New Orleans. Her old man, Ross, ain't had Sue but a year. The crumb crusher's daddy was wasted in a card game . . . cotch, I think. Ross ain't got Sue really tight. He's too strict. Don't see why he ain't blowed her 'fore now . . . 'cept maybe she done got freakish to his foot in her ass. She's been an orphan since twelve . . . Saw her daddy waste her mama with a butcher knife. That's it, Slim. Oh yeah . . . Happy birthday!"

Bitsy got to her feet. She laughed scornfully. "That dizzy ho is aching to be a lady ho . . . wants to cop lots of book learning . . . cop nice proper speech and all that phony shit. Ain't that a bitch?"

I said, "Ain't it! Thanks, l'il sis."

She scurried back to the cash register.

Phil said, "You ain't gonna get the chance to play for Sue the airtight way Ross bird-dogs her. He'll shoot or stomp a mud hole in your ass."

I said, "Phil, I gotta figure an angle to make her hit on me. You know, give me the first lick. How about laying a rod on me . . . to back me up?"

Phil shrugged. "Not now, pally. I got to think about it, nigger. It's gonna take more than my flash and your bedroom eyes to make that ho give you that lick. Guest of Honor, you better just handle the licks you gonna get here in the joint before daybreak . . . Lots of qualified black and white hoes gonna be here letting their hair down."

The joint's band drifted in and started tootling and blowing a few practice riffs on a bandstand beside the bar.

Single mud-kickers, black players and their interracial stables, started to park far-out pimpmobiles up and down the block. They peacocked into Pretty Phil's all decked out in psychedelic threads.

Phil introduced me to the strangers. Many of the players I knew. The inside of my mitts were flaming from the palms I slapped. It was phantasmagoria. They wantonly danced to the funky band's erotic pound. In the red-lit murk, there was the counterpoint bedlam of profane ribaldry as they loaded their skulls with cocaine and the bubbly. The mirrored globes revolving in the ceiling speckled their faces with flashing light. The meld of their perfumes was a near suffocating cloud. It was like Dante's Inferno updated.

By four A.M. the joint was claustrophobic. I had gotten several ho licks and birthday wishes galore. But I felt lonely and blue, like a joker in a haunted house. I was in the basement of a pit. The superfox ho target hadn't shown, and I was still just a welfare case of Phil's.

I retreated into a booth in the absolute rear of the joint next to the ho crapper. I eyeballed the front door with the radiant zeal of a weasel.

Bubbles, the Dane, had taken station near the front slammer. She was coldly sweeping her eyes over the crowd like the stomp-down security guard Phil had cracked she was.

Phil threaded his way to my booth. He leaned into my ear and whispered harshly. "You blind or something, pally? That redhead white ho at the bar is pinning you and about to come on herself. Latch on to the ho's eye! Honor the lick! It's catching time, nigger! Flow and glow, pally." He shook his head and moved away.

I was turning my head to yank the package he'd fingered when Miss Superfox herself pranced through the front slammer. Alone! Appropriately, a drumroll of summer thunder announced her entrance. A shard of lightning flashed like a klieg light behind her.

My ticker rioted. A delicious stealing lust electrified my genitals. She was dap and down in a black chiffon chemise vine. A white mink stole was draped casually across her shoulders. She smiled frostily as she sidestepped through a gauntlet of cracking and hitting players to a stool at the bar.

I had to string together a stealing tune based on Bitsy's rundown. Like I said, I was just a welfare case. You know, with no stable and power like Phil. With a power base I would've blitzed her. You know, dazzled her witless. At least I'd have to fake a bankroll. I wrapped Phil's welfare handout of "C" notes around a wad of play money.

I was forced to take my shot at the Superfox's soft underbelly. I'd have to be like a mirror reflecting her secret needs and dreams. She'd have to see me as the means to these gratifications. It was a long shot and dangerous all right since Ross, the gorilla, was her boss.

The dynamite package had seated herself beside the redhead Phil had fingered. I sipped rum and spied the bar through my booth's wall mirror.

Phil stood near Bubbles at the door. He hawk-eyed me and Miss Superfox with a salty look on his girlish face. The perspiring band blazed out raunchy toe-tappers. The dancers whirled and boogied as if energized by demons.

The redhead, Lucille Ball's look-alike, rocked on her stool to the music. The tipsy flat-backer turned her back to the bar. She zeroed in on me with hooded blue eyes. Her dress was hiked nearly to her moon, and aimed at me.

The Superfox got off her stool and wafted Chanel No. 5 up my nose on her way to the john. I saw Phil peer out the front Venetian blinds. He spun and frantically winked his eye. A moment later, a brute-faced colossus, togged to the teeth in a shocking pink ensemble, stopped his six eight or nine feet of bulgy muscles past the top of the front door.

Despair descended. It had to be Ross, and my stealing dream was lost. He strode the length of the joint with his Neanderthal skull swiveling as he shook down the joint. He was two booths from me when he stopped. He leaned into a booth. Moments before, a pint-sized loser in a tattered vine had slid into that booth beside a brunette silk girl. Phil had introduced her to me as one of the girls employed at Aunt Lula's cathouse.

The loser copped a heel in terror. The alabaster beauty fled the joint like Ross had goosed her with an ice pick. Ross went out behind her.

The front door was still closing when Superfox came past me from the crapper. I suffered the thought of what a miserable break it was that she didn't dig him leaving with the white girl.

I was sitting there regretting that she didn't have to just pee when a loud-mouthed ho called Miss Bowlegs eased out of a booth ahead. She went to the bar grinning. She whispered into Sue's ear. She swirled on her stool like she was making a country break for the door. Instead, she frowned and hailed a barmaid like she was settling in for some sho 'nuff tippling. The fire-and-brimstone patron saint of pimps was in my corner all right.

Black Sue was tossing double shots of scotch down her gullet as fast as the harried barmaid could lug them. She had a lulu lump under her right eye. The sight of it shot a thrill my way. Had the gorilla's right cross and the wire from Miss Bowlegs put him in the cross to blow the fox to me?

After a band break, Phil went to the bandstand and rapped with the leader. A barkeep unveiled my birthday cake and hors d'oeuvres on a table set up on a corner of the bandstand.

Lanky Phil adjusted the mike up to his jib and shouted, "Pallies, damper the rapping! My main man, Candy Slim from the Big Windy, is gonna cut his cake and rap a taste."

I rose and moved out to applause. As I passed the redhead, she grabbed my arm and slurred, "Candy, as a pair we'd be dandy. Huh?"

Sue leaned in close, with bright racist eyes, to dig my response to the symbol of black women's pain and mortal enemy. I nearly swooned with joy to play my opening card.

I batted the alabaster hand away and cracked icily, "Look, you jive flat-backing zero bitch, stay out of my face! Don't fuck with me, huh!"

The redhead, moist-eyed and humiliated, sagged and about-faced to the bar. Sue's eyes glowed with admiration as I boogied away to the bandstand. The band struck up a raucous "Happy Birthday." I polished the next card I'd play as I cut the cake. I went to the mike and swept the crowd with doe eyes, then I slipped on a mournful mask, faking the emotions of a dude with hurtful blues.

I stood there in the silent red haze for a dozen heartbeats before I pitched, "Sugar babies, most of you are hip that I just got up from a fall. Only Phil, my homeboy, is hip that I lost my bottom rib and our daughter in a car crash a month before I split the joint. She was a thoroughbred, my woman! She stacked up long scratch in the kip for me. I'm happy if I don't look it. Sugar babies, you've lifted me like a blow of crystal. I know that somewhere way out there past the sky, my woman and angel kid are happy this morning, happy 'cause I'm honored here by blue-ribbon people. You can't stop a stepper, sugar babies, and I love ya!"

I went back to the booth through a chant of "Happy Birthday, Slim!" backslapping, and warm congratulations. Black Sue followed me into the booth like a doll on a string.

She just sat there studying me, with our eyes locked. It was a long time before she said, in a satin drawl, "Sugar, Black Sue is gotta tell you, you something else, and then some. Them sweet words relating to your dead daughter and bottom lady nearly got me bawling like a squealer. Slim, you something else! . . . Lemme buy you a taste."

I leaned and whispered into her ear, "Later, I just want to be with you."

I decided to play Sweet Willie all the way. I feather stroked the inside of her wrist with my fingertips. Her bottom lip trembled. I glanced past her. Phil glared cutthroat murder at me and whirled out the front door into the rain. That was good. Phil could pull my coat if the gorilla drove up. I pressed her hands against my lips and gazed into her eyes. She swept a fearful glance over the joint.

I crooned, "Baby Sue, let's flee to a taste and some talk in my crib upstairs. I'm convinced something boss is happening between us . . . Doll face, maybe you need me . . . Let's find out."

She said seriously, "My old man is Jabbo Ross . . . You hip to how he is . . . about me?"

I said, "I've heard."

She murmured, "And you ain't leery?"

I said stoutly, "I'm not into pussy. Sugar Pie, I'm game to climb up the devil's mother-humping ass with you this morning."

She laughed shakily. "Well, let's go, sweet Chicago Slim."

I dropped the twister to Phil's pad on the tabletop and said, "We might give some jokers in the joint diarrhea of the jib if we split together. I'll cop some blow and wine and follow in a moment." She scooped up the key, squeezed my hand, and started to slide her awesomely curved rear end from the booth. She braked and dug into her midnight cleavage and excavated a roll of bread, peeled off a "C" note, and shoved it into my shirt pocket.

I felt my scrotum spasm. I was zeroed in on her now, reading her tactics. She was playing star ho test shit on me. I wasn't uptight about that. After all, she had to check out my pedigree. She was at the very least unconsciously considering me as her new boss! I leaned and eased the booby-trapped "C" note back down between her epic peaks. The plum-colored tips gleamed through the chiffon gauze.

To certify my pedigree, I slipped on a mask of terminal pain and cracked a mild reprimand. "Sugar Sue, you got to know what starts right, goes right . . . Up front, I'll spring for the nit-shit refreshments."

I flashed my fake bankroll with the solid funny-money guts. I said, "You're sweet to be concerned about me just out of the joint and all. Now you can stop worrying about the little things."

She smiled crookedly and split. Phil came in from the rain with his silky black hair shining in wet ringlets. He sat down across from me.

He said, "Nigger, the joint sure as hell didn't damper your speed. Too bad it's Ross she's gotta dump." He slipped a thirty-eight snub nose from his waistband. I took it off beneath the tabletop. He rammed a balloon of blow into my shirt pocket as he got to his feet and said, "Some ploy to prime the ho . . . I'll send up some sauce."

I got up and said, "Sugar baby, I know you're royal blue, and I'm your horse if I never win a race."

He said as he moved away, "Pally, kiss my yellow ass 'til it's royal blue."

I left the joint and stood on the sidewalk for a moment engorging my lungs with rain-spiced air. I went next door through the hotel entrance to the dim musk of the lobby. An elderly desk clerk with a brown clown face nodded toward the stairway. He winked obscenely as he made a lopsided circle of A-OK with pudgy fingers shiny greasy with barbecue he was gnawing. I slowly ascended the foot-mauled stairway carpet to polish the next stealing card I'd play.

I went to the suite door and pressed my ear against it. I heard the erotic confection of Dinah's voice dripping her sugary "I'm Confessin'" from Phil's hi-fi. Then I heard the muted thunder of the shower.

I turned the knob. Surprised that she hadn't locked the door, I stood at the threshold gazing about Phil's pimp dream arena. I've guested at the Chase in St. Louis, the Ambassador East in Chicago, the best at the Drake in the Big Apple. Phil's white and gold ho trap paled the other cribs.

I chained the door, then moved beneath a crystal chandelier in the entrance hall to the airy carpet of the living room. I familiarized myself with the three rooms so I could move about with assured ease when she joined me. Then I hung my jacket in Phil's closet and slipped on a gold satin smoking jacket. I selected a blue silk pajama top for her.

I went to the living room's white satin sofa and arranged my bag of coke into sparkling columns on the blue-mirrored cocktail table. Across the way she suddenly opened the bathroom door. She stood still-lifed, naked, holding a towel. Her blue-black curves shimmered like sealskin in the amber glow. I got an instant, throbby, quality erection. Small wonder. I had a helluva time willing my hoodlum organ limp again.

She looked so young, the crafty eyes now softened and fawnlike. I realized she was like me and every other street-poisoned nigger spawned behind the invisible walls of ghetto stockades. She was trapped, vulnerable, but hurtingly human beneath the tough facade of leopard rage and bravado. But in the cruel nature of our special entrapment, and my survival, my comrade in pain was ironically my prey. I would have to scrape to the raw nerve ends of her emotions, put her on the rack to steal her.

I stood up to break our trance. She patted the towel against her splendor coming to me. I kissed the tip of her nose and the plum blossoms of her swollen nipples. I toweled off the wet sheen as tenderly as a mother would a baby.

I heard a feline purring in her throat as I blotted her vulva. I assaulted her mouth with teeth and tongue. She squealed in the painful thrill of it. I vanquished her tongue in a sugary duel. She seized me. She clung to me moaning gutturally.

I finger-stroked the invisible forest of fuzz on her buttocks, the insides of her thighs, across her shoulders, the pits of ecstasy beneath her ears, the valleys behind her knees. I never once touched her skin. I was certain each one of the supercharged zillion hairs was jolting her with the electricity of inexpressible excitement.

I swooped her off her feet down to the couch, where I slipped her into Phil's pajama top to break the action. Then I moved away across the cushions. She pursued. To escape, I rolled up a "C" note and dipped my head to snort up a row of "coke." I passed the paper horn her way to cool her fever and watched her snort up a row of blow.

I'd have to be cool to outplay her. Otherwise, I'd wind up at dawn with just a belly full of pleasure. No money. No ho. No contract!

I watched her go into the bathroom to rummage among her things. I watched her squat and extract a thin package from her vaginal stash. She detoured on the way back to the hi-fi in the corner. She belly danced her way back to the sofa to Hamp's "Flying Home." She dropped the soggy package from her cat on the cocktail tabletop. I guessed it was a sting she hadn't checked in to daddy gorilla. She fell on to the sofa with her head on my lap. Her big pony eyes were all a sparkle, gazing into my face.

She sighed, "Slim, I feel so good with you . . . really good! You feel groovy, too, with me?"

I gently knifed a fingernail across her kneecap. She shivered.

I cracked, "More than I ever remember . . . with somebody else's girl."

I knew it was an off-key crack as soon as it exploded against my ears. She leapt up and went to the floor-to-ceiling windows. She stood there staring out at Miss Rain tap-dancing a zillion diamond feet against the windowpane.

She said over her shoulder, "I like rain . . . Jabbo thinks it's a drag."

I had broken the stealing spell and unveiled the threat, the reality of the gorilla. I checked myself just as I decided to join her to recast the spell. I had to keep her coming to me to cop.

I lit up two bomber sticks of dynamite gangster. I blew several blasts of pungent smoke her way. The vision of her four-inch cone of thick bush between the sculpted thighs was lost for an instant. I wondered if my chance to steal her was lost.

She turned and walked over. I handed her a joint. She pranced back to the window hitting the joint. I unwrapped her toilet paper package a bit to peep. A dime-sized circle of jewels winked at me from an inner wrapping of "C" notes and fifties. It had to be the sting from the husky sucker in the Buick. Had she baited it out like that to excite me out of position when I cracked to see the contents?

I restored the wrapping and went to the bedroom. I was on my way to the shower when the doorbell chimed. I opened to the old joker on the desk with Phil's Jeroboam of bubbly and glasses. He nearly tripped himself gazing at Sue's caboose as he went to the cock-tail table with the tray.

I said, "Thanks, Pops, I'll take care of you when I come down tomorrow."

He made that lopsided circle with his fingers before he split.

I speed showered and added on French cologne with its dusting powder. I heard the pop of a cork. I slipped into a pair of Phil's crimson satin pajamas. I stood before a mirrored wall and brushed my hair until it shone. My reflection, with my widow's peak and slumberous eyes, made me look a bit like Satan. Well, anyway, at least like one of Satan's pets afire in the red pajamas. I was beginning to feel like a pimp again, all right. I hit the gangster roach and stepped into the arena.

She was lounging on the sofa with her legs agape. As I passed her, I paused to check for trance. She sipped and gazed up at me over the rim of her glass. She was on her way under again. Her eyes were getting dreamy and smoky hot again.

She gave me a glass of wine. I dipped a finger in and painted her lips. I licked and sucked it off her mouth. She pressed her cheek against my crotch. She kissed the imprint of my organ as I moved to sit on the cushions at the other end of the sofa. The big vein on the side of her neck was swollen and jerking.

"What a womb sweeper," she exclaimed.

She lunged to my side and glued her curves against me. I held her and silently sipped my wine for several minutes like a joker with his mind on a private expedition to secret things and places. Sweet Dinah was dripping "I'm Confessin'" from the hi-fi again. She nibbled through the satin to my nipple.

It tickled when she whispered into my chest, "You thinking about her . . . your dead lady . . . ain't you?"

I said, "No, babykins . . . a living lady . . . my mama."

She snuggled closer and said, "What's she like? Tell me about her."

This was my cue to push her emotional buttons to prep her for the contract. I sang the tune slowly from the bitter roots of my own pain and poisonous ambivalence for Mama.

I stage-whispered, "All right, but something bothers me, babykins. I can't figure why I'm not with Mama . . . after the joint . . . on my birthday. Jesus Christ! She'd be so happy. She was a country girl . . . barefoot 'til she was sixteen. My old man ambushed her with sucker sweet talk and popped a squealer in her gut . . . me . . . They split the Big Foot cotton slave scene and hit the Big Windy kitchen slave scene in nineteen eighteen. You know, white folks' mansions and hotels. They had discovered the Promised Land, all right.

"Right off, my old man copped some loudmouthed suits . . . His introduction and sample of white pussy . . . It freaked the nigger out! I was six months old . . . Must have been a sonuvabitching stumble block to his nightlife chumping around. He and Mama fought like pit bulldogs one early bright . . . He pranced home stone broke with his fly fouled with 'come' . . . his mustache starched with cunt juice . . . He beat the puking, living crap out of Mama . . . He bounced me off a tenement wall to close his act . . . He split with a cardboard suitcase and his pearl grey spats flashing in the zero wind. Mama had a nice round ass with a Watusi face and lollipop knockers. Why, shit, any other young country broad equipped like that would've dumped a squealer and split to the bright lights and some high-class dick."

Sue trembled against me as she finger-stroked my temple. Her eyes were damp with empathy.

". . . But Mama was a blue-ribbon Mama to the bone . . . She bundled me in an old army jacket . . . took a curling iron and some grease to the streets . . . dressed hair door to door for a lousy half buck a shot . . ."

She pressed her glass against my lips. I took a sip, then raced my tongue a few laps inside her mouth.

"Tell me more, Slim! Tell me more!" she pleaded.

I went on with the painful narrative. "Well, somehow, she put together a survival kit that took us through the soup kitchens, bread lines, apple hucksters on every corner nightmare of the Great Depression. I was nine . . . maybe ten when she got tired, I guess . . . You know, the struggle must have been a bitch of a drain . . . Anyway, a big, ugly black galoot chased her until she caught him. He wasn't her style . . . She was a sucker for good-looking bums . . . like my old man.

"I remember how Mama would cringe away from Henry's kisses . . . She hated him. But he was the only father I ever knew . . . and I loved him! Mama dreamed I'd be a lawyer . . . Henry swore he'd see to it . . . opened the plushest black beauty shop in Rockford, Illinois, for Mama.

"She got the hots for a two-bit hustler one day who brought his pretty face her way . . . dropped in to get his nails done. Just like that, she split with him back to the Windy. I cried until my guts dry locked . . . The pretty bastard was so cruel to us! Tried to turn her out. Mama cut him loose finally. But it was too late for me . . . I was already street poisoned. Maybe I got a secret hate for Mama hidden deep in my soul, because Henry died from a broken heart after she split. Maybe that's why I'm punishing her. Why I'm not with her on my birthday. Maybe I want her dead and stinking like Henry. Maybe that's why I don't want to see her happy for even one day."

The Mama rundown worked like a mojo. She leapt to her feet with eyes brimming tears. Her body was twanging emotion.

She said with righteous heat, "Slim, you all fucked up in your head about your mama. You ain't hip she's a saint? Shit, lemme tell you about my chippie-ass, dead and stinking Mama—that half-white Creole bitch treated Papa and me like dogs. You know why? 'Cause we had black skins. She only married him 'cause he had a farm and a few bucks. Her ass was dragging. She was played out as a chickenshit flat-backer ho in Baton Rouge.

"I got an older sister that thinks she's white—she got the new shoes and pretty dresses. She was high and mighty Miss Anne. I had to wait on that bitch hand and foot or get my head busted. Papa and me picked the motherfucking cotton and slopped the hogs. Papa and me did the cooking and the washing. Mama and Miss Anne kept their asses pretty and prissy like muckety-muck white bitches. Papa caught her sucking a white man's dick in the barn. He killed her and the white man."

Her voice broke, staggered the bitter rim of hysteria. "I'm glad he did. I'm glad she's in her grave, dead and stinking. I'm just so sorry poor Papa had to do it."

I pulled her down beside me and said gently, "What happened to your papa?"

She made a strangulated sound of anguish in her throat and stared into nowhere like a sleepwalker. She almost whispered, "I found him in a pond. I didn't know what the thing was at first there in the bloody water. They beat, shot, and axed him to pieces . . . poor Papa!"

She collapsed in my arms. Great heaving sobs of sorrow racked her. I rocked her in my arms like an infant until she got herself together somewhat.

She said, "Slim, will you do something for me?"

I said, "Sure, anything."

She looked me dead in the eyes. "Go over there and call your mama."

I said, "What the hell am I gonna tell her?"

She said, "Tell her you love her, Slim. Make her happy . . . Make me happy, Slim."

She followed me to the phone, embracing my waist from behind. I put through the call and awakened Mama in Milwaukee. I talked to Mama for twenty minutes. She kept whispering to me to introduce her. I did, and she and Sue hit it off swell for an hour.

Before Sue hung up, she made me happy. She said to Mama, "Honey, we will be dropping in on you one day soon." Then she looked into my face for a long moment and said, "Kiss me. I wouldn't bullshit your mama. I'm your girl!"

I kissed her for real.

She said, "Close your eyes, Birthday Bunny."

I did. Shortly, I felt her fingers at my pajama coat. I opened my eyes. I fingered the stickpin. She slapped the roll of bills in my hand.

She said, "There's fifteen hundred there . . . now let's fuck, Daddy!"

I led her on off to bed. We made love until noon. I wondered whether I could beat the gorilla to the draw when I staked my claim to his woman. I couldn't have legal pimp title until I faced him with her since he was available in town. We lay in Phil's emperor-sized bed, steeped in the odor of our love juices. We made our plans to hustle tough for a year before we would make a home for Carla, her daughter.

Finally I said, "Let's get up and do what we have to do."

She said, "You mean catch a plane out of here?"

I said, "No, I mean let's go drop the bad news on Jabbo. You know, and get your things."

She propped herself up in the bed and squeezed my face with her eyes before she said, "We don't need to take a risk like that. You don't know Jabbo. I boosted everything I got. I can steal a new wardrobe. Let's just split, Daddy. Okay?"

I eased Phil's snub-nosed rod from between the mattresses. I said, "We've got to do it right . . . We've got to face him . . . This rod makes us equal."

She sighed and slipped out of bed to shower. I lit a joint and tried to figure just how to accomplish the mission and leave it in a per-pendicular position. I mean alive! I called the desk to locate Phil. He answered from Bitsy's room.

He said sleepily, "Pally, you and that ho are in serious trouble if you ain't got no understanding. Miss Bowlegs pulled Jabbo's coat that you and Sue were fucking around."

I said, "She's my girl. We're on the way to break the news to him. Then we're splitting. I'm gonna check out the afternoon plane schedules."

Phil chuckled, "Bring me my piece, nigger. Did the ho give you claiming dough to cop a forty-one hog that runs like a scalded dog?"

I said, "Look, Phil, I need your piece to brace that nigger. Who's selling the hog? And what's the bite?"

He said, "It's my old hog, and the bite is a measly grand to you, pally. C'mon and cop it so you can ease in and cop the ho's clothes and hit the road."

I said, "Phil, you drunk? You think that nigger will let us ease in his crib like that? If he's not there, he'll be staked out for sure."

He said, "He ain't in town. I dropped the word in the street that you and the ho had split to Akron. I tailed him to the highway myself . . . Get here, nigger, and take care of your business!"

I hung up woozy with relief.

Phil's forty-one Fleetwood I bought was a black beauty. At a distance, it was almost as clean as his new forty-six. We made a fast raid and copped Sue's clothes. Late that night a rainstorm struck at the edge of a town in Illinois. I was dozing on the seat beside her.

Suddenly she said, "Daddy, look!"

She pointed at a skeletal white man with a slicker draped across his gaunt shoulders, cape style. There was something eerie about him. He was standing motionless.

His stark white face glowed in the storm. He looked like a statue of Count Dracula.

As she cruised the Caddie past him, she said excitedly, "That paddy gives me wild stinging vibes. You take the wheel when I pull over. I'm going back and shake him down. Daddy, he's sweet and loaded. I feel it!"

She pulled to the curb two blocks away and started to open the car door.

I said, "Sugarface, pass him up . . . Don't play for him. I got a helluva bad feeling nudging me about him."

She sprang out of the car and slammed the door. I slid across the seat fast to open the door to physically stop her. I mean, that joker really turned me off. She turned twelve feet away. In an explosion of lightning, her doll face was radiant with stealing lust. She blew me a kiss and waggled "bye-bye" with her fingers. You know, like a little kid who is just going to the grocer on the corner.

I'll never forget how I felt as I watched her tiny figure disappear, forever, in the storm. In the distance, I saw what looked like the tail-lights of a pickup truck flash on like bloody orbs and disappear into the raging blackness.

For 36 hours, I didn't shave, eat, or bathe. I searched everywhere. I called the local police station.

I disguised my voice. You know, laced it with a Slavic accent, pitched down to a guttural register to make it sound indigenous to the area. I reported that I had seen a nigger girl kidnapped in a pickup truck. I gave the description of the ghoul in the slicker. I hung up when asked my name. I went to the local newspaper office and bought a subscription to their rag. I gave Mama's address in Milwaukee.

I was in a blind fugue of shock all the way home. I had no recollection of the trip. My room and it's mementos of my junior high school days were intact. I looked about it and guessed that Mama had preserved it as a kind of shrine to cushion her loneliness and guilt for her hots for that ho-faced sonuvabitch long ago.

There on the wall, a faded blue felt banner. On the dresser top, a gleaming trophy I won for the hundred-yard dash. There, against the wall, a rickety Flexible Flyer sled. An eight by ten blowup of me at five seated on the lap of a padded department store Santa Claus.

Holy Christ! . . . What a rack of torture she must have been on. Blaming herself for my terminal street poisoning. Suffering that I wasn't that upright, silver-tongued mouthpiece she'd dreamed me to be.

I got really blue and sad that fate had dealt us a black card from the bottom. I was torn down with that, and Sue, to make it worse. I went to Mama's bedroom. You know, to comfort her, to tell her I loved her, like Sue had begged me to do. Mama was on her knees praying for Sue before a homemade altar. What the hell could I do but get down on my knees beside her and pretend to pray?

At midnight, that first day, I unpacked Sue's bags. I sat on the side of the brass four-poster and opened her album of pictures. Ah! There she was, barefoot in a rough cotton dress, squinting in the sun as she lovingly held a puppy against her cheek. A shot of her father, riding a mule, a black-as-midnight tiny guy. His face was seamed and ruined by stoop slavery in the cotton fields beneath the inferno sun.

Her octoroon mother, the Baton Rouge strumpet, appeared surprisingly beautiful and innocent in a white dress. The closet monster was posed with Sue's porcelain-skinned sister before the backdrop of the scabrous death barn watching a polka-dotted sow suckling piglets. Ah! Sue and her daughter, with Sue's string bean Cajun husband, standing proudly in front of the gumbo greasy spoon they owned before the gorilla came Sue's way and turned her out.

I closed the album and went to bed. I hadn't closed my eyes all night when Mama called me for breakfast at eight. Two days later, the first paper from Illinois arrived. Sue had made news all right. Horrendous news! I uncontrollably jiggled the paper as I read the account of her end. The fiend she had played for was an escaped nut from an asylum for the criminally insane. He had taken her to an abandoned farmhouse. He had crucified her and tortured her to death with his teeth and a hunting knife.

Two teenagers, hunting rabbits out of season and drawn to the presence of the fiend's stolen pickup truck, had peeked through a window and saw her nailed to a wall. When the rollers showed, the fiend was in a drunken stupor on the floor beneath her corpse.

Mama and I flew to claim the orphan's body. I can't forget that sunny afternoon I walked into the morgue to identify her—that is, what was left of her. The attendant pulled her out of the cooler bin. He jerked away a bloody and filth-pocked rubber sheet like she was dog meat. I gazed down at her and retched.

That inhuman cocksucker had hacked and scraped off her crow breast mane of shining hair that had leapt from her temples in spectacular, voluptuous waves. Her skull was crisscrossed and gouged with knife slashes. Her doll face was unrecognizable, except for the stable pony eyes staring blankly into mine. The cupid bow mouth had been lumped hideous from punches. Her teeth were bared in a macabre grin. Her body was measled with cigarette burns. Her honey-dipped breasts were ragged stumps. The satin belly was disemboweled from her breast bone to pubic hair. Her fingers were missing, and the butt of a cigarette protruded from her vulva. I staggered away, vomiting all the way to the sidewalk.

We buried Sue that week from Mama's church. We got the location of Sue's infant daughter's foster home from Sue's address book. Mama shipped Sue's stuff to Carla.

In the limo, on the way from the cemetery, I told Mama about Sue's plans and dreams to square up and open a restaurant to make a decent home for Carla, her daughter. Mama broke down and wailed like a crumb crusher. Small wonder. Mama had lost her dream too, a billion tears ago.

Thirty years later, whenever I see a pygmy fox with indigo, velour skin and pony eyes, or see a shimmering mane of crow breast hair, or hear a smoky voice, I get a lump in my throat remembering Black Sue.

# LONELY SUITE

I tossed restlessly in the emperor-size bed in the Big Windy. The moon-drenched branches of a wind-mauled tree outside the bedroom window cavorted spectral shadows about the suite. Raucous March gales screeched off Lake Michigan. I felt a bleak loneliness, a nameless apprehension. I chain-smoked as a blond console in the living room issued Ellas's new hit wail about the loss of her "Little Yellow Basket."

I was startled from my counting of the gold satin ruffles on the bed's canopy by the jangle of the telephone on the nightstand. I froze and stared at the phone for a long moment. Three A.M.! Was it Phyl, my one and only mud-kicker calling from the slams? Had some mugger on Sixty-third Street slugged and robbed her? Had some trick maimed her?

I picked up with vast relief to friend Gold Streak's frog-in-a-log voice. "How ya doing, Slim?" he shouted above a background of honky-tonk pandemonium.

"Great, Streak," I said. "You must be balling at Small's Paradise, or maybe at the Cotton Club?"

He laughed. "Your ass, buddy. I'm back in Chi! Stole the finest three-way silk bitch in the Apple. I'm celebrating my birthday at Wimpy's, then Tracy's for a taste. C'mon!"

I said, "I'm waiting for Phyl. Want me to pick you up in your wheels later?"

He said, "No, Jim, I got the cabby with me that drove me from the Apple." He hung up.

I went to the bathroom to freshen up for my lady due to check in. I was just a nineteen-year-old pimp novice. I wasn't scoring a big buck from the streets with one flat-backer. I wasn't really the suite's tenant. I had agreed to hawk-eye (from my modest pad down the hall) and occupy the suite during prime burglar time. Streak had a fear that some scuffler would shim his pad and cop his five dozen pairs of stomps, hundred vines, and assorted personal treasures. Streak had been on business in the Apple for a week. Dope business.

I brushed my teeth and felt pangs of worry and fear for Streak. The nasal sludge in his voice was the tip-off that he had strung himself out on his merchandise. Worse for Streak was the street scam that he was long past due in payment for supplies of dream shit from you know who.

I went to a bedroom window and idly glanced down a street. I saw a group of white couples and a pair of sharply dressed Mutt and Jeff Italian dudes alight from cars in front of the hotel. Apparently they were catching the Nat "King" Cole Trio's last show in the hotel cabaret.

I went to the blue-mirrored bar and mixed a Cuba Libra, overweighted with rum. I heard Sparky, a pimp friend with a noisy mob, go into his suite across the hall. Then I put Savannah Churchill's "Time Out For Tears" on the turntable. I heard a gentle knock on the door. I thought it had to be Phyl. I felt irritation that she had lost the key I had entrusted her with.

With casual reflex, I unlatched the door. It swung open. The stack of records clattered to the carpet. I stared slack-jawed at the Mutt and Jeff Italians I had glimpsed on the street muscling into the suite. Jeff pushed the door shut. They stood like sphinxes, royal blue overcoated, dap and deadly, inky eyes hooded staring at me. I couldn't ask them what they wanted. My terror and the stench of the oppressive cologne made me nauseous, mute.

My vocal chords were paralyzed. My lips banged together sound-lessly as I obeyed the imperative command of porcine Mutt's head dip at the sofa. I collapsed onto the sofa with gluey palms. Mutt shoved his blue fedora back off his face and sat on the coffee table facing me. My ticker boomed counterpoint to Savannah's tearjerker.

Jeff stage-whispered something in Sicilian. Mutt grunted and belched a stinking gust of garlic and pasta. Jeff materialized an auto-matic piece from a shoulder holster as he cat crept into the bedroom. Jeff came back into the living room scowling. He sat down on the coffee table beside Mutt. They glared at me.

I found my voice to say inanely, "What's the trouble?"

Mutt said, "Who are you, kid?"

I said, "Bobby Lancaster."

Jeff leaned and tapped my forehead with the snout of his piece. He said, "Now, Bobby, we got urgent business with Otis . . . very important! Where is he?"

I bit my lip thinking fast. They exchanged a few rapid words in Sicilian as I procrastinated. I caught a bit of it for I had grown up next door to Sicilian pals in Rockford, Illinois. Their rap had sounded like, "squeeze the skinny asshole." Jeff stomped his heel down on my bare instep. My eyes leaked water. I almost tinkled in my pajamas with the jolt of pain.

I was about to blurt out the info when the truth hit me. They had to waste me since Streak was a walking dead man already. They couldn't leave me alive. They couldn't risk my possible identification after they hit Streak! I closed my eyes and thought about Mama. I remembered how she had wept and pleaded with me to stay in school, to avoid ruin and early death in the underworld. I thought about unforgettable, dazzling Opal, my childhood sweetheart. Now it was all over. I was finished at nineteen.

Savannah's song was winding up. I heard Phyl's key in the lock. I groaned. She was finished too. I opened my eyes. Jeff raced to the side of the door with pistol ready. Phyl opened the door. My friend

Sparky, the pimp, and his dozen-odd mob of hustler pals were spilling out of his suite. Mutt released his grip on my hair. Sparky embraced Phyl's waist from behind and nuzzled her ear.

Sparky glanced at me on the sofa and hollered as he waltzed Phyl into the room, "Young Blood, my man!"

The wild mob followed Sparky and Phyl into the suite. Jeff dropped his piece tight against his hip. He jerked his head at Mutt as he stepped into the hallway. Everybody froze and stood staring at my mussed up condition.

Mutt snarled, "Clear the way!" He moved from behind the couch waggling the automatic. The crowd parted to make an aisle to the door.

Sparky said, "What the fuck is going on, Slim?"

I said, "Everything's cool now."

Mutt went past the muttering, menacing mob into the hallway. I went to the window and watched Mutt and Jeff drive away. I knew their unfinished business wouldn't take them far from the hotel.

While Phyl was helping me clean myself up in the bathroom, Sparky came to the doorway. He said, "Baby bro, you better cut Streak loose."

I said, "Streak and the mob split to an after-hours spot down the street."

Phyl and I split to our pad. I called Tracy's joint several times and got the busy. I put in an emergency call. No dice; the line was out of order. I paced the floor and glanced out the window every few seconds. Streak was a cinch to be ambushed if I didn't risk my life and go to Tracy's and pull his coat. But I was leery!

Then I got it! I'd send Phyl in a cab. I went to the bathroom doorway and watched tiny Phyl cold creaming off the ho makeup from her baby face. I couldn't send her. Her face looked like a trusting child's in the mirror.

She smiled at me. "Daddy, you feel like making love?"

I kissed her hard and said, "For real, baby! Soon's I get back."

It was a man's mission. I dressed in dark clothes, rammed my pistol into my belt, and told Phyl not to leave the pad and split. I went to the roof and tried to spot the Mutt and Jeff Buick staked out. I went down the fire escape to the alley. I started down the black pit alley toward Sixty-third Street for a cab. Two blocks away! Platoons of rats scampered and squealed across my path.

Deep into the nightmarish tunnel I saw the black shape of a car oozing toward me with lights out. I snatched out my pistol. It slipped from my sweaty hand and bounced on the alley floor. I dropped to my belly behind a trash bin and retrieved it. My shaking hand pointed it at the windshield of the car moving toward me. The car stopped ten yards away. It was a Cadillac!

I got to my feet. As I passed the startled white dude under the wheel, I saw a Sixty-third Street ho laying head on him. I was dizzy with relief when I stepped into Sixty-third's carnival of neon and whistled myself into a cab.

On the long trip to Tracy's on the Westside, I remembered how I'd met Streak. Junior high was out for summer vacation. Opal Grady, my first sex mate sweetheart, and I were having a picnic lunch in the park one July afternoon. We noticed an older young guy in tattered, dirt-streaked clothes. He'd amble out of the bushes to get a drink of water from a nearby fountain every few minutes. Each time, he'd sneak a ravenous glance at our layout of food. Opal suggested that we share with him. I followed him to his pad in the bushes. I had a helluva time convincing him to accept the invitation to join us.

He introduced himself to us as Otis Banks. Guess we were the first to meet him formally when Otis the orphan had swung off that freight train from Dixie three days before. He had oodles of warm, comedic charm. He hooked Opal and me right away. I remembered there was an extra room at home. He shot Mama down within an hour after she met him. Mama copped him a gig as mop technician at city hall. I loved him like the brother I never had.

But he was restless, had been street poisoned down in Memphis. A year later, he split to the fast track and left a sentimental note for Mama and me. Through his rare visits and rumors, I kept in touch with his street career. He had hooked his heart to become a pimp. His black patent leather skin stretched across the Cro-Magnon features was a slight handicap. The major handicap of his tender dick, compounded by his secret pedestal reverence for foxes early on, had chilled his long shoe dream.

He peddled low-grade eights and sixteenths of smack and cocaine, instead of dick, out of crappers in junkie dives for several years. Then he copped the big bag. He bleached a gold streak down the center of his processed hair to cop his moniker and to match his gold hog. And now, I thought, as my cab pulled to the curb at Tracy's, Streak's golden street bubble had popped.

Tracy's doorman peeped at me through the spy hole and opened the steel door. I walked into the acrid smoke haze and wall-to-wall night people. The Seeburg jukebox was firing neon and Hamp's "Flying Home." I spotted Streak at the crowded bar. As usual, he was a loudmouthed, animated symphony, decked out in puce and gold threads. The Carole Lombard look-alike blond fox he'd stolen in New York was beside him, draped out in threads that matched his own. Next to the fox teetered the fat, black New York cabby. I muscled through jitterbugging fanatics in the aisle toward Streak.

Streak hollered above the din, "Set up every motherfucker and cocksucker in the joint, and give the mice some cheese, the cat some cream on Gold Streak!"

Tracy, the ex-pimp bar owner, was behind the bar slaving with his barmaids to serve the thirsty crowd. As I moved in close, I heard Gold Streak high jiving and needling perspiring Tracy. Just as I reached Streak's side, Tracy blew his cool.

He rammed his bitch face close to Streak's and shouted, "Get outta my ass, Gold Streak!"

Streak just threw his head back and laughed. He threw his arm around me.

I said, "Streak, let's split!"

He said, "Not now, Slim." Streak said to Tracy, "Nigger, you funky as a two-dollar ho behind that bar. My woman is got enough scratch between her titties to buy this cracker box."

Tracy said, "Fuck yourself, Jive Ass!"

She whipped out a bale of "C" notes from her outrageous cleavage and tossed it onto the bar top. You could have heard two cockroaches fornicating on Mars in the sledgehammer silence.

I leaned into Streak's ear and whispered, "Jesus Christ, get yourself together. Streak! Let's split! Two Outfit Aces are out to hit you!"

Streak's face ashened.

Some joker expressing the collective passion of the clientele shouted, "Girl, I oughtta stick you up."

Streak glanced about anxiously and drew a Magnum pistol. He scooped up the bundle into his overcoat pocket. We threaded our way to the street. The three of us got into a cab. Streak checked into a fleabag hotel several miles away on the Westside. His fox went into the shower. He slumped down on the side of the bed. I sat down beside him.

He moaned, "Slim, it's the end of the world!"

I said, "Get in the wind, Streak. It's a big world."

He shook his head and whispered, "It ain't no more. Slim, it ain't no use. Those cruel bastards have already shrank it to the size of a morgue slab unless I get all them 'gees' I'm into 'em for."

I stayed with him until dawn before I said good-bye. I split to Cleveland the same day. A week later, I got the news he had been shot a dozen times pulling his Caddie from a rented garage on the Westside.

After ten years and a slew of blown hoes, I came back to Chi on my uppers, strung out on "H" and one junkie ho, Phyl. Immediately as I checked into a third-rate Southside junkie hotel, I discovered there was a dope panic.

Old Man Sparky, reduced to boosting for a living, was a tenant in the hotel. He steered me to some three percent smack that kept me and my girl from being sick. His once round handsome, yellow face was wasted and scabrous. Sparky lay in his greasy bed coughing up tubercular phlegm as he ran down conditions in town.

He said, "Slim, you've come back to a motherfucking graveyard. Ain't been no decent dope in the street for a month. Better split with your ho to Detroit or the Apple."

I said, "I have to get scratch to split. I'm almost on 'E'. Any quality shit in Gary? Any on the Westside?"

He shook his head and said, "There's some choice brown Spic dope here on the Southside. But you gotta have the connection and the long scratch to copy at least a quarter of the piece, at double the usual bite."

He was racked with a seizure of coughing for several minutes. He continued. "If Phyl is become the thief you think she is, maybe you can cop some of that decent dope if your ho stings big, soon! The only connection is a cold-blooded bitch, Pretty Opal. She's cribbing up in the hotel where we used to crib. The bitch is got Gold Streak's suite."

I said, "Sparky! Is she a blue-black stallion with legs like Grable, tip-tilted nose, a big round ass, and bedroom eyes?"

He nodded and screwed up his face. He said, "Slim, if you can shape it up an angle for her, you better do it fast. Smarter still, Slim, don't play for her. Ina cross fire you could get in the family way. With lead!"

I said, "Why?"

He said, "'Cause she's one of the reasons for the present dope panic. Last month she toured the beds of the three top dealers in town. She laid her poontang and bullshit on 'em just long enough to get hip to their operations. She laid her suction cunt and a sawed-off shotgun on a snot-nose heistman called Wee Billy to rip off their merchandise. Those niggers got hip and sho' nuff salty. That ain't all.

I heard she just got back from fucking around with ugly-ass Klondike, the biggest dealer in Detroit. Klondike is the most treacherous nigger that ever shit between two shoes. The wiser is she and her dwarf sucker will be wasted any day now. I'm gonna worry about you, Slim, if you cut into her."

I was stunned. Visions of clean-cut Opal, the teenage ball-blaster, rushed through my head. Oh, the spicy spoor between her satin thighs. The rose garden, the manicured jade of lawn, moonlit in the rear of her palatial home. Her hypnotic eyes caressing my face as I volleyed my blood-bloated weapon into her incredibly fat sex nest. I remembered the musical laughter of her elegant mother and socialite guests wafting on summer air just before Opal's father's bellowed rage spooked me into the wind just as I orgasmed. No, Opal the dealer wasn't—couldn't be—my Opal after all.

I said, "Sparky, I don't know Opal the dealer, so I got no angle. The Opal I knew was a stone young lady, with top-drawer parents. Why, her old man had the largest black furniture and appliance store in the country. Guess I'll run over to Milwaukee and try to score."

Sparky hiked himself up in the bed. He said, "It's the same Opal. You know the bitch. Her old man got busted. He was the biggest fence for heisted jewelry and hijack whiskey there ever was. He made the front page of the Defender a coupla years after you split to Cleveland. You know the bitch! You gonna try to score for some of her Spic dope, ain't ya?"

I nodded.

He said, "Take real good care, Slim. Lay a pinch on old Sparky if you do."

I felt my monkey sandpapering my guts as I went to my pad. I decked myself in the best threads I had. I didn't care if Opal had turned into the fucking devil. I had to cut into her and score for some of her brown Mexican ambrosia. I felt sorry for her in a way. But what the hell, I thought. Opal had realized the fondest dream of thousands of black street people past and present. She was ensconced in the top black hotel, in its most lavish suite. Dope Queen Opal had arrived!

I called her. She squealed at the sound of my voice. My numb junkie scrotum tingled at the sound of her contralto voice.

I stared into the opaque eye of her suite's peephole as I rang the chimes and heard the metallic clamor as she unbarred and unbolted the door. It swung open. I stood on the threshold scanning her face. I was amazed that in the sorcerous pink glow, she appeared to be the same uncorrupted schoolgirl she had been. I rushed into her out-stretched arms. We embraced and kissed for a helluva time before we sat down on the freshly upholstered gold silk sofa. Her Rubenesque curves shone through her diaphanous negligee like indigo satin. Her fabulous legs were curled beneath her Yoga fashion. Her waist-length hair shimmered black like a miniature waterfall. She gazed into my eyes as she pushed back my sleeve and finger-stroked the spike tracks on the inside of my wrist.

She said softly, "Bobby, maybe I shouldn't have invited you to see me. Your eyes have changed."

I laughed hollowly. "It's jungle warp, angel, that's all. I can split if I make you leery. I don't heist or mug for my medicine."

She shaped a little smile. "Come to think of it, you wouldn't have to. You had a sweet bitch of a hitch in your hips on the down strokes. How many girls do you rule?"

As I stroked her spike tracks inside of her thigh, I said, "One thief at the moment. But I'm taking applications from the qualified . . . even demonstrating an advanced bag of strokes from the hips and the brain. Doll face, five grand or so, in good faith scratch, would entitle you to the special introductory opportunity to get all of those goodies and paradise too."

She nodded her head toward a gigantic oil painting on the wall and murmured, "I painted that. That's Wee Billy, my teenage sweetie. I'm the ruler type too, Bobby."

I studied the nude image of her Lilliputian slave with the

cast-iron balls to rip off dope dealers. He had a snarling, girlish, banana-hued face and a steel wire body. His sex tools hung grotesquely huge. He seemed afloat in an ocean of flame red clouds.

She said, "I'm his Jocasta in a way. He loves me with reverence like the mother he never knew. But he fucks me with no hang-ups at all. He's devoted, obedient, and cold-blooded like the Doberman I had when I was ten. I could command Billy to waste that tie salesman in the White House, and he'd do it for me. He wouldn't ask why. He'd die trying. He loves me!"

She smooched my forehead as she rose and spun Eckstine's "Jelly, Jelly" on a mahogany console. She went to the bedroom. I glanced about the sparkling suite. I hoped Billy wouldn't show before I copped some medicine. I shivered remembering Gold Streak and that long-ago morning when Mutt and Jeff jacked me up. She came back naked. My first thought was that she would try to swindle me out of some swipe and/or cap, until I noticed the shooting works in her hand.

She crooned, "Darlinkins, take off your clothes and let's do up."

I did. She cooked up a spoon and drew a shot up into the dropper. I was so frantic to bang some quality I missed the vein twice. She took the spike and hit me good. I was engulfed in salubrious waves of euphoria. She cooked another batch and drew up a shot. Then she got on her knees on the carpet with her big round rear end between my knees.

She said, "Sugar, hit me in the ass."

I daggered the spike into a vein. Her plum-tipped anus blossom quivered when crimson flooded the dropper. She groaned ecstatically as I bulbed and drained the dropper empty. She turned and kneeling, cocooned my scrotum with her hair. Then she rested her head in my lap as she had when we were children.

She whispered, "Sweetheart, I'm so lonely and afraid, afraid for Billy. He's a whole day overdue from business in Detroit."

I stroked her head and said, "He'll show, doll."

We shot dope, and I kept her company until two A.M. Christ! She needed me as much as I needed her dope. I put on my clothes to split. Phyl would be coming in off the streets needing a fix.

I said, "Doll face, you've been a jewel. I don't beg charity. Do me a favor and sell me an eighth of shit for my girl and me to wake up on."

She went to the bedroom and came back and gave me a fat glassine pack of smack and said, "I'm giving you that for old times' sake. Call tomorrow to check on me."

I kissed her. I was at the front door when the phone rang. I paused and studied her face when she picked up and listened. I had never before, nor since, seen such bombshell terror on a human countenance. She let the receiver bounce on the carpet as she collapsed beside it. She stared up at me with tragic eyes that will haunt me to the grave.

She whispered raggedly, "Detroit niggers dumped him in an alley, like a varmint . . . Wee Wee is dead! . . . They chopped off his swipe and balls . . . stuffed them down his throat . . . sliced off his ass. Cocksuckers! Hammered a steel pipe up his ass! Poor Wee Wee . . . I was the only mama he ever knew . . . Oh God! Help me, Bobby!"

I thought, what a black widow mama Wee Wee drew. I turned and took a couple of steps across the carpet to comfort her. Then it hit me! Billy had been tortured before death released him. An eighteen-year-old, or just about anybody, would puke out his gut secrets under a torture quiz. Like Opal's address. Billy's killers could be on their way for Opal. They would wipe out any hapless soul found with her. I fanned out the door.

I went down the hallway for the elevator. I almost soiled myself when an olive-tinted black pimp, with the moniker of Dago Frank, sporting a broke-down pearl-grey lid, stepped out of his room in the shadow-haunted corridor behind me and hollered, "Hello, Slim!"

I was in the street with my hands on the door handle of my ride when the sentimental, interior sucker sent me back for Opal. The door was still open. She was still transfixed with horror and terror on the floor. I yanked her to her feet. I scooped up her coat. We split the suite.

Since day had decapitated night's bummer head with a bright golden ax, that suicidal sucker in me forced me to get her off the street until night encored. At my pad, Phyl split to Sparky's room with her spare of the quality smack.

Opal and I shot up my dope and sat on a couch drinking syrupy refreshments as we planned her escape from the city when darkness fell. In the drawn-draped dimness of my pad, Opal's face was so soft and innocent. I found it difficult to believe that almost fifteen years had passed since our puppy love affair.

I said, "Baby, ain't it a bitch how we both struck out? Remember how we used to dream and brag in the park, on your front porch swing on those summer nights? You were going to be the first superstar black painter for openers. Then after that, if you were in the mood and the dough was right, you'd hit Hollywood as an actress and nudge Nina Mae McKinney and Dorothy Dandrige aside."

She sighed, "Yeah, square-ass dreamer me. And you, Bobby, you were going to be the first black Clarence Darrow . . . to make your mama bust her heartstrings with joy. Sure, I remember the dreams I spun. It put the hurt to me through the years to get hip that there was never even a rainbow . . . much less a pot of fucking gold!"

I said, "Something puzzles me. I fell from a family nest broken when I was just a squealer. My old man bounced my noggin off a tenement wall when I was six months old. Mama lugged the load solo. Before I met you I was street poisoned. We lived across the street from a ho house. I'd sit in my room and watch the pimps, in silk shirts and yellow toothpick shoes, come to get their money with satchels. Damn! I'd get excited when they'd pack their hoes into Duesenbergs, Lincolns, and Caddies and cruise away on joy rides. I ached to be a pimp when I was just twelve.

"But your old man and mama were tight and strong together.

You grew up in a fine, respectable neighborhood. Your family nest was peaches and cream. I can't understand how you wound up in the sewer with me . . . Why, when I lost touch with you, you were on the turn for a cotillion ball for debs. You drove your own new Chevy convertible. You were decked out in the finest threads from Marshall Fields, fabulous Lili Anne suits. You were even voted, in high school, to be the most likely to succeed in the rat race of life. I've heard that your father took a fall fencing. I can understand that must have been a bitch of a crimp. But what happened, beautiful, after that to flush you all the way down the toilet? Where's your mother?"

She sighed and poured it out as she wept: "Poor Mom and Dad. He died in Joliet prison. Funny thing, the three of us were so happy before Mom started social climbing, started tearing her asshole out, and Dad's, to compete with the status shit bastard muckety-mucks of so-called nigger society. Dad was a religious, good man, with only a grade-school education. But he had lots of business sense. Mom came from a cushioned background. But so naive. She couldn't know that Dad's store couldn't support her extravagances toward the end. He loved her so much, more than his God. He let it override his morality, his basic common sense. He became a crook to finance her madness. He destroyed himself because he couldn't say no to her.

"But I paid for all of it when I went to dance at the Grand Terrace the next week. I picked up a dapper nigger with the softest voice and sweetest face I ever saw. It was Muskegon Shorty, the cruelest ass-kicking nigger pimp that ever fell out of a cunt. He turned me out and worked me sixteen hours a day, every day for two years at Thirty-fifth and State streets. A nigger in a craps game blew him out of my life."

She sobbed uncontrollably. I gave her a couple of reds and rocked her into fitful sleep. We lay in each other's arms on the couch. Night fell as we clung together.

She stirred and said, "Bobby, I'm going to my grandma down in

Mississippi. I'll be safe. I can't go without stuff for heavy jones. I've got to get my stash of smack from the suite."

She got up and slipped on her shoes. I begged her not to go. When I couldn't turn her around, that sucker inside me made me volunteer to take her back to the suite. Maybe she was a cold-blooded bitch.

But she said, "Bobby, darling, I can't front you like that."

Guess she still had a teenage sucker spot in her ticker for me, too. She stood in the door and kissed me good-bye. She pressed a slip of paper into my palm.

She said, "Bobby, it's my grandmother's phone number and address. Let's keep in touch. Oh, by the way, I'll stash you a taste of shit under the face bowl in the public men's john on the lobby floor. Bye, baby."

I watched her go down the hall through the lobby to the street. Jesus Christ! I felt bad to see her go in trouble. Around six A.M. my jones prodded me to check out Opal's john stash of smash she'd promised.

I drove to her hotel where I saw a cluster of people on the sidewalk at the front door. There was a city meat wagon on the street. My heart rode my throat. I parked and walked over to a bellman.

I said, "Who cashed in?"

He said, "Pretty Opal."

I turned away so he wouldn't see the spill of tears down my cheeks. I went and sat in the car and watched the wagon's attendants load her corpse and truck it away into the night. I sat in the car for two hours before I got myself together. Then I went and checked the face bowl stash in the men's room on the lobby floor. Poor Opal had OD'd before she could keep her promise.

A month after Opal OD'd, Phyl blew to Milwaukee with a dealer holding a big bag of high-grade smack. It jolted me to be ho-less, broke, and alone. Except for my monkey, I had pawned all my double-breasted ho-catchers. I mean, I was ragged as Yakima. I broke the long shoe rules and played peel-off stuff with a couple of fellow losers to bribe the monkey from kicking the vomit out of me. The three of us cruised up chump change in a stolen ride for a week before we got busted.

That last midnight we spotted a trick ramming it into a drag queen in a pickup truck. We leapt out and flashed our fake roller badge. We were inspecting their IDs and peeling off the green stuff when a squad of heat showed with shotguns. I caught a slat in the joint on the coal pile.

A month later, I said, "Shit! I ain't gonna do this bit."

I did a black Houdini to Indiana on Good Friday. For the next thirteen years, I yo-yoed up and down the pimp string in a dozen states. I was up the string in Cleveland with three girls humping in cathouses when I decided to encore Chi. Naturally, I called to find out if that suite was available. It was!

I drove into town. I was disappointed and depressed to see a junkie coasting in the lobby when I checked in. I followed a bellhop, with my bags, to the suite's door. He unlocked it. I had made it! I was finally a tenant of the suite. I was so excited as I paused on her threshold. I entered her. I was betrayed. I was depressed! Her once bright complexion was brassy and pocked hideously with an ancient smog of nicotine. She was sleazed and greasy from the legions of junkie joy-poppers who had fouled her rotten with their shooting galleries.

Oh, I was turned off. I despised her leeched-away glory. Her bed raiment was splotched and frayed. Her panoramic windows, once so clear as to be almost invisible, were now cracked and glaucomitized by soot and pigeon offal. They now afforded only a myopic view of Sixty-third Street's festival of lights. My impulse was to desert her instantly. But, inexplicably, I could not. Even in her ruin, she held me captive!

I used the phone to keep in constant touch with my girls in the cathouse salt mines. The loneliness in the bleak suite became almost unendurable. Since I was an escaped fugitive, I felt imprisoned in the suite.

As the Christmas holidays approached, I was beginning to think it was a wrong move back to Chi. But I had Rachel, my youngest star, coming in to keep me company through the holidays. I sent the bell captain in my ride, camouflaged by counterfeit registration with plates to match. He delivered the package. He set her bags down and split.

We embraced, and she kissed me with zest. But I saw her face spasm with disgust as she swept her emerald-flecked eyes about the pad. It was a comedown all right, from the glamorous high gloss of cribs prior to where I had headquartered.

I took her to Milwaukee for a riotous several days of cabarets and parties. Too quickly, the holidays were over. To bypass loneliness, I decided to let her kick street mud on Sixty-third. I hoboed heroin's express train to you know where for company while she was away humping from seven P.M. to four A.M. She was stand-up, four-square in my corner for almost a month. I mean, her bread was consistently up to par when she checked it in.

Then one morning at dawn, quite a bit past her customary show time, I noticed an odd, preoccupied radiance about her. Now, I knew that the stem where she worked was infested with young ho masters. But I was Rasputin; well, at least Svengali.

After all, I had liberated her from a third-rate greasy spoon and turned her out. I had transformed her from a grease-splattered chippie nobody into a chick and irresistible lure for tricks. But anyway, I couldn't quiz her. I couldn't tip any sucker emotional shit to her. That could blow her fast to one of the gaudy novices on the stem.

The one morning, close to eight A.M., she pranced home, reeking of alcohol, and her head bad. Now, I won't try to describe my agony on the ego rack waiting for that sugar-faced bitch. Let's just say, my pain was inexpressible. Oh, I wasn't in love or anything close to it. It was worse! I mean, I was threatened by the pimp chattel thing. The threat of losing her could maim my delicate ego at thirty-five.

Well, anyway, I watched her from the bed in the bathroom mirror as she brushed her teeth. I glanced at the thick wad of bills she'd flung on the bed. Christ! It was short. Was she splitting my bread with some downy-cheeked peacocker? It was a helluva struggle not to cross-examine the truth out of her. She darted a culprit look my way in the mirror.

I said, "Baby sis, the scratch is light . . . you feeling all right?"

She shackled her breath for an instant. "Yeah, Daddy, I feel fine. The track was lousy slow all night. That fifty on the bed, I got from a trick an hour ago. Except for him, I'd a shot a blank."

I said, "Damn, baby, you're a star. I better get on the phone now . . . Maybe I won't put you down another night out there. . . . Why, it's easy, I'll cop you another gig in a top joint. . . . Maybe up at Grace's in Montana."

I reached for the phone to test her.

She whirled and pleaded, "Please, Daddy! . . . I just had a bad one . . . first I've had . . . Let me stay on the track here . . . near you."

She hadn't conned me. I knew she was fucking around. Now that I knew, I couldn't even ship her if I wanted to. I had made a mistake when I yanked her from the ho house. I had put too much trust in my power over a turnout. I had ignored the compulsive desire of any turnout to flee the master who had put her new slick image together.

I watched her from the sofa as she got herself together promptly for work that night at seven. She dipped her head to my crotch. I thought she would, as tenderly as always, kiss my swipe good-bye. But she raked her teeth down the shaft and moved away. She paused at the door and shaped a Mona Lisa smile. She waggled good-bye with her fingers like a little kid.

With her eyes averted, she said softly, "Daddy, I'll be very late . . . maybe noon . . . got a long 'C' note trick, a regular . . . Gonna turn him around four this morning."

I went to the window and watched her slog her booted delicate feet through the snow until she disappeared. Christ! She was delectable in her curve-hugging scarlet-hooded coat, white fox-trimmed. What a precious property! I thought about the countless hours, energy, and care it took to turn her out, to buff off her rough edges, to make her a top package. What a heartbreaking bitch if I blew her!

I remembered her noon check-in and how she had slashed my jones with her teeth. She had always been so lovingly gentle before in the good-bye ritual. I thought, maybe it was the tip-off that I had blown her. I felt a gnawing ache in my gut that she wasn't coming back. At least not as my girl. My head roared at the thought of blowing her. I decided to Dick Tracy her a bit to cushion me against the pain and shock if I lost her. Damn, the pimp game was torture for an old pimp, I thought, as I got the bell captain's borrowed ride and drove to the stem.

I parked with a view of her work corner at Sixty-third and Cottage Grove. I sat and watched her flip car tricks until midnight. I was thinking I might have been wrong that she was shaky, when a new white pimpmobile parked in front of a bar on the corner. Then I saw a dapper young dude get out and pose on the sidewalk.

He was a baby all right, no more than twenty-two and pretty as an Eurasian bitch. His processed hair coruscated like a black satin helmet in the neon splash. His pink vine trousers shimmered on his greyhound lean frame beneath his beige vicuna topper. Rachel raced to him. She kissed him and clung to him possessively. She dug frantically in her bosom and gave him what could only be trick bread.

I had lost her all right. I knew it by this pimp prance of triumph as they went into the bar. He had taken off the ho's bread and most likely had massaged her tonsils with his swipe to cop legal pimp title. He had stolen my ho! I was physically ill, devastated, as I pulled from the curb.

My hands trembled on the wheel as I drove like an automaton through near collisions to the hotel. My feet felt like anvils as I went down the hallway to the suite. I collapsed on the bed in my overcoat, where I lay in a trance until daybreak. I just stared into the ceiling mirror at my haggard reflection, at my graying stubble of beard.

The phone rang. My heart leapt. Maybe she had quarreled with him. Maybe he had beaten her up so badly that she needed me. My hand trembled as I picked up.

One of my young, hero-worshipping bellboys said, "Mister Slim, your lady and Dandy Maurice, the young pimp, just checked into one-forty-three. I . . . uh . . . thought I'd pull your coat."

I laughed. "Thanks, li'l bro, guess he's tricking to steal her ass backward with his dick."

He laughed unconvincingly. I hung up and cooked a "C" and "H" speedball stew for breakfast. I shot it and mulled the situation. The pretty baby sonovabitch was playing a steel down game all right. He had contemptuously lugged her beneath the same roof with me. He was down there playing sweet protective Willie to tighten final screws, to strengthen her and his new contract. He knew how shaky and blowable a stolen bitch, fatigued from the track, was, before she faced her ex-boss to cop her clothes.

I decided I had to save face, give them a show, not a production, when they swooped down with the bad news. At eight A.M., I called the elderly ex-pimp bell captain to the suite. He came in and sat on the couch beside me. He was embarrassed in his empathy for my situation as we put together my show.

I said, "Roscoe, in the next two hours get me the finest young fox you know to come here and play my ho. Send up a Jeroboam of Mums bubbly and crystal goblets on a jazzy tray. Get me some fresh drapes and a sparkling throw rug to cover that worn spot in the carpet near the door."

Roscoe said, "For three bills, I can get Helene, the prettiest white call girl in the Loop to spend the day. Nothing like a blond white bitch with movie star looks and body to drool that punk and chill the shit of that nigger bitch you done blowed. That rest of what you want, you'll have by ten o'clock."

I gave him two bills and went to the bathroom to sanitize myself. I scrubbed myself raw. I shaved my face raw. I brushed my hair and teeth until they shone. I decked out in gold silk pajamas and lavender silk robe with gold slippers.

At nine, the housekeeper brought the throw rug and installed new peach drapes. Fifteen minutes later, a bellman brought the Jeroboam of Mums, nestled in a solid silver ice bucket with crystal glasses on a silver tray. At ten fifteen, I opened the door to Helene. She was decked out in a sable-trimmed white walking suit. A bellboy set down a huge matched pair of chic luggage. She looked like a seventeen-year-old double for Kim Novak, only taller and more pulchritudinous.

She stood in the doorway and gazed at me like I was Tyrone Power. She said in a pro's sweet husky voice, "Oh, Slim! My Gawd, you're so handsome."

I nodded toward the sofa and said, "Helene, I'm bullshit proof. I'm not buying pussy; I'm buying whatever acting skills you've got. Understand?"

We sat down on the couch. I gave her three bills. She flicked her tongue across the back of my hand and hooded her electric-green eyes. I ran down her role. She opened her bag and extracted sheer black baby-doll pajamas. She stripteased naked before me to the racy beat from the console, Brook Benton's and Dinah's "You Got What It Takes." She slipped into the baby-dolls. She flung herself into my lap and licked my nipples.

I said, "Helene, get your clothes off the floor, unpack, and hang everything in the closet. The curtain will be rising any moment now."

Helene was painting my toes scarlet to match her nails when the chimes sounded. She opened the door, stepped aside, and said, "Hi. Come in."

Maurice and Rachel hesitated, awed by the pastel vision for a mini-instant. Their coats were slung across their arms. The tic in Rachel's cheek jerked as it always did when she was excited, or jolted. They stepped in. Helene came back to the sofa to resume the painting of my toenails.

Rachel cowered behind him as per the protocol for a defected ho. Her tic was rioting on her jaw. Maurice had his right duke rammed into his suit pocket. He darked his dreamy, but resolute grey eyes across my robe in a check out for cemetery bulges. To tout her pussy, Rachel had probably conned him that she'd opened my nose. Which she had in a way.

I said, "Helene, this is Maurice and Rachel. Maurice, no doubt, you already know who I am by reputation."

A shadow of surprise moved across Maurice's face that I knew his name.

I nodded toward a love seat across the way and said, "Take their coats, Helene, and pour them a taste."

He led Rachel to sit on the love seat. Helene poured champagne from the coffee table. She took glasses to them and reached for their coats.

The doll-face infant said, "We're not staying long." He looked at me and said, "Slim, how about a few words in private?"

I thought, *Damn, that motherfucker's eyelashes are long and lacy.*

I managed a suave smile and said, "Sure, Maurice, we can rap while Helene is helping Rachel pack her things."

The girls went to the bedroom. He came to the sofa and sat down beside me and sipped champagne. His fresh unlined face was earnest as he looked me dead in the eye. I remembered my own pristine face, and I felt a pang of sympathy that he was dumping his youth and life down the rat hole of pimping. I had the insane desire to preach him out of his poisonous trance. But I knew it was too late.

He said, "Slim, you've been my idol since I was a teenage street bum down at Thirty-first and State. You had a new player's ride every year, the finest ladies, the most fabulous threads, and so much class. I swore a thousand times I'd never chump off my life in a steel mill like my old man. I was gonna pimp like you, be admired and respected by the niggers on the corner like you. Why, Slim, I took a fall at sixteen and your name was ringing like a motherfucker even in the joint. I took a vow I'd stop stealing and pimp like you, live the sho' nuff good life like you, be famous like you."

He paused to light a cigarette. I heard the girls clearing out Rachel's piles of makeup bottles and perfumes. I thought, *Ain't it a bitch for this young chump that hoes, pressure, and age will rip off his rose-colored glasses and kick his ass.*

He continued, "Slim, Rachel gave me a lick first. I swear I didn't hit on her. She gave me claiming bread and freaked off in my bed. I had no choice. But you know the game . . . It's cop and blow. What I'm trying to say is . . ."

I cut him off. I said, "L'il bro, you don't need to run down hearts and flowers to a stoned ice player. I celebrate when I blow a ho . . . hones me to cop two in her place."

The girls came into the living room with Rachel's bags. We stood up and shook hands. I leaned and whispered, "Son, take an old player's advice. Don't hold on to the brass ring until it turns to shit."

He looked puzzled for a moment. He said, "Use your phone, Slim?"

I nodded. He called a bellman. Rachel kissed my cheek as they were moving out with her bags.

She murmured, "Good-bye, Daddy."

I shut the door, went to the sofa, and sat down beside Helene, curled up seductively. I said, "You were great, Helene. The curtain has dropped. I want seclusion."

She kissed me and went into the bedroom to pack and dress. I went to the window and watched the bellhop load Rachel's bags into Maurice's pimpmobile. Then I watched it disappear with the star that Slim built. I wanted to bawl like a crumb crusher to see her go, to see all those big potential bucks hit the wind.

I stood there at the window long after Helene had gone. Finally, I cooked up a dangerously big shot of dope and tried, unsuccessfully, to jolt myself numb from the pain of losing Rachel and to escape the excruciating loneliness of the suite.

I packed my bags and dressed. Then I sat on the side of the bed and lit a cigarette. Suddenly, bitter, frightful déjà vu seized me. I recoiled like a mad man. I cringed away from ghostly shadows cavorted by the wind-flogged branches of the ancient tree outside the bedroom window. My wild crying echoed through the suite as I wept for Mama's tears and her dreams I'd stomped on. I wept for Gold Streak, Opal, Maurice, and Rachel. I wept for all my wasted years and wasted friends and girls between treacherous Mutt and Jeff night when I had lay in the suite wanting for the child-ho Phyl to check in. I bathed my face and called the bellboy. On the way out of the suite, I paused and looked back at her ruin.

As I turned away, I whispered, "Good-bye . . . good luck, Old Girl."

# SATIN

Notorious Etta "Satin" Lewis tooled her El Dorado from Chicago like the Furies through ranting wintry winds. At last she arrived in Milwaukee. The car skittered on the icy street as she pulled it into the curb to park. Her fabulous legs trembled with tension as she walked across the snow-clogged sidewalk to ascend steps.

She squared up her shoulders inside her white mink coat, pausing on the stone steps at the door. Her black satin Cover Girl face was sad as she paused. She stared at a brass plate on the door engraved: PASTOR MARY LEWIS. Stricken, she fought tears as she heard the deacon's eulogy rising above the moving "Amens."

"Mother Lewis, our pastor, our saint, is gone on her trip into divine infinity. Her doctors reported her ticket home was stamped heartbreak and hypertension. This church, this city, all of us have lost a powerful warrior for love, compassion, and human rights." The shaky voice broke. "I tell you, if I didn't believe deep in the pit of my soul in God's divine wisdom and plan, I'd ask, 'Why, God? Why? Why did you call Mother Lewis from us?' Oh, Lord, it hurts so bad! Please, Lord, light the way, show us heavy-hearted sheep the way to do without her! Help us, Father!"

Satin stiffened her backbone and thrust her chin high as she opened the door to step inside the crowded ghetto church.

Late.

She removed her coat, slung it across her arm. Burning with

embarrassment, she went down the aisle through a silent sea of faces to a front pew near the flower-banked open casket. She sat down heavily between Ora, her older sister, and Mimi, her seven-year-old daughter. They clung to her as she kissed them. She squeezed and held their hands as the deacon sat down behind the pulpit.

The choir sang the final hymn of the service. The string bean deacon stood and smiled sadly, looked at the family survivors, and dipped his head toward the casket. The black-clad trio rose and went to the casket. Pews emptied at the rear of the church as mourners formed a line to view the body.

Ora and Mimi broke into hysterical weeping as they looked down at the seamed, finely-sculpted black face of Mother Lewis. Satin's lips trembled as she stared at the ruined image of her own face. She struggled to keep her vow not to cry, not to let the self-righteous mob of squares, who hated her for breaking their Mother Lewis's heart, see her emotions bared.

She remembered that just five years ago her mother's snowy hair had been jet-black with only a few sprinklings of gray. She remembered the town's outrage, the disgrace, the pain in her mother's eyes when she cried and begged her not to leave town with dope-dealer pimp, Chicago Razzle Red. Despite her courage, Satin wept. Beneath her wild sobs she whispered, "I'm sorry, Mom. I made a mistake . . . Forgive me."

She embraced Mimi and Ora and led them back to sit and watch, through a fog of tears, the congregation filing past the casket for their final glimpse of their beloved Mother Lewis. In a trance of sorrow, Satin took the arms of Ora and Mimi and followed the pall-bearers with the casket to the sidewalk. The funeral director helped her into her maxi mink coat.

A crone poison-monger in the crowd spit venomously into the snow and stage-whispered, "The Lord's surely gonna put a curse on Satin's imp and her luxuries for killing Mother Lewis."

Satin turned to flog the crone with her masterwork of street profanity, but the funeral director gently, but firmly, shepherded her into the family limousine behind Mimi and Ora. Satin slumped on the rear cushions of the limo in shame for her near loss of control, all the way to the snow-choked cemetery. The grief-stricken sisters and Mimi wept convulsively at the rim of the grave as Mother Lewis's remains were lowered into the earth.

Satin told herself again and again, "I didn't kill her! Red did! Red took me away! Red killed her!"

The limo took them to Satin's car. Satin drove to the front of the brownstone house where she was born. She wanted to go in and visit for a while, but she was sure the memories inside would break her down again.

"Etta, aren't you coming in for a moment, at least for coffee?" Ora asked.

Satin shook her head. "Sorry, Ora, I've just got to get back to some very important business."

Ora leaned across the seat and kissed Satin before she got out. Satin rolled down the window. Ora stuck her head inside the car. She watched Satin place a gold necklace from her purse around Mimi's throat.

"Please, Et, don't go! Stay this time with me and Aunt Ora for always." Wide sable eyes, set in the moppet's tearstained black cherry face, were pitifully hopeful.

Satin kissed her, held her to her bosom, and whispered into her ear, "Not this time, baby, but I'll be back soon to stay. I'm even going to bring you a wonderful daddy with me. I promise. Soon. Aunt Ora is not well, so be a good girl. Help with dishwashing and keeping the house clean and stuff. Okay?"

Mimi pressed herself close against Satin as she said, "I already do, Et. I can even iron my dresses for school. Gimme some idea when you coming home. Auntie and me gonna really need you with Granny gone to Heaven."

Ora looked into her sister's eyes as Satin said, "Before spring, angel . . . in a couple of months."

Mimi's voice was muffled in her bosom. "No jive, cross your heart and hope to die, Et?"

Satin pressed her lips against the crown of Mimi's head. "No jive, cross my heart and hope to die, darling."

The moppet's eyes were radiant as she blotted tears with her coat sleeve. She slid reluctantly from the car as Ora opened the door and slammed it behind her. Satin turned the ignition key, watched them go across the sidewalk hand-in-hand, turn, and wave.

Ora opened the gate to the white picket fence. She turned and said, "Wait a moment."

She took Mimi into the house. Shortly she came back to the car with a letter.

Satin said, "Oh, by the way, Ora, will you take your phone off the hook this evening until morning so the usual check-up calls from Red can't come in from Chicago?"

Ora nodded, gave Satin the letter, kissed her again, and returned to the house.

Satin opened the letter, frowned, and groaned as she read it. She gunned the Caddie and parked a mile away in front of the site of her expensive dream, the dream threatened by the letter on the seat beside her.

She scanned the three-story red brick hotel. Its bleary neon sign blinked out: SIMS'S HOTEL on its weather-sleazed facade. The room curtains were frayed and dingy behind grimy windows.

Her eyes were bright with excitement as she visualized how the building and its rickety room furnishings could be transformed under her ownership. She saw a sandblasted building looming freshly gleaming: ETTA'S INN rippling neon fire above the lobby entrance.

She noticed an elderly waitress and ancient Mister Sims behind the bar in the hotel's tavern, stooped and laboriously serving a sparse crowd. She imagined a gigantic mirrored sphere whirling from the ceiling, spraying pastel jewels of light on sex pots in bikinis, serving wall-to-wall people in the posh womb of ETTA'S CABARET.

Instead of queen of Razzle Red's eggshell empire of hoes and dope, she thought, I'll be queen of black Milwaukee's business-women. If, her heart sank, I can take off that ton of geeters this week, if plans stand up. "Don't panic," she told herself. "You'll convince Mister Sims to extend the option to buy for at least until next week in case the big score is delayed."

She slid from the gold Caddie to the street. She felt hooligan winds maul her as she crossed the sidewalk into the bar. She magnetized all eyes as she took a stool near the door.

Old Sims came to her with a solemn look and purple lips pursed. "Hi, my dear. Let me kiss the prettiest waitress I ever had . . . my sympathy for the passing of Mother Lewis."

She said, "I appreciate that, and I'm always thrilled to see my darling Mister Sims," as she warmly kissed his mouth.

He said, "How about your Daiquiri on the house?"

She smiled and shook her head. She thought, I better stroke him with tactical chitchat before I crack for the extension.

She glanced at the darkened kitchen cubicle at the rear of the room as she said, "How is Mama Sims? Seems kind of odd not to see her back there turning out the best soul food in town."

His droopy, hound face was serious as he mused, "She's poorly . . . she missed you, the customers missed you . . . came in here by the droves asking about you. Most of 'em stopped coming, went to jam the Apex down the street instead when that slick Red Nigger stole you. Lost Timmie too . . . died last week."

She said softly, "I'm so sorry to hear that. Poor sweet boy. What happened to him?"

"He whiskeyed himself to death," he said harshly. "Started soon's you left town three years ago. Woulda broke a murderer's heart to see Timmie, the Sheik, shabby and falling down drunk. I woulda swore, and him too, you two was gonna marry and settle down after you had his baby. Guess you did what you wanted to do."

She bit her lip. "Please believe me. Mister Sims, Mimi was an accident. I . . . uh . . . never misled Timmie. He was fun. I liked him. He begged. But I always told him I just couldn't marry him." She heaved a sigh. "I'm really, truly sorry Timmie didn't get over me."

A customer at the end of the bar knocked his beer mug against the bar. The old man patted her wrist and shuffled away. She removed a gem-encrusted cigarette case from her white mink bag and flicked flame to a lavender papered cigarette. A panting Lothario, in a baggy, checked suit, sprang from a booth with a flaming lighter. Too late.

The old man returned and cupped her hands in his bony paws. He leaned close and said, "You get my broker's letter?"

She nodded and pouted. "I almost cried, Mister Sims. You just have to extend my option to buy the hotel. I may need until next week to get the money. I want to prove something in this town for Mimi . . . for Mama."

He shook his gray head emphatically. "Wish I could, but I can't. My broker's got me the best offer I've had. Me and my old girl have lined up our plans to go 'round the world and enjoy ourselves. Our time is short. I gave you sixty, then thirty days to buy. Too bad you don't have the credit for the financing. You'll find something else you want when you're ready." He shrugged. "The buyer is paying cash like the letter said, when your option is up in two weeks. It's out of my hands now. I've been fair, been your friend since you left your mama's home in your teens."

She stood and said fiercely, "Mister Sims, I'm going to buy this hotel. I'll be back with the cash before my option expires." She turned for the door.

He said, "Wait, Etta!"

She turned back to the bar.

He whispered, "Lemme tell you a secret. I hustled moonshine, busted out craps, been shot, stabbed, and poisoned, even prison before I squared up in this hotel thirty years ago. Listen to someone that loves you. You gotta be honest and straight to be happy. Don't put your young beautiful self in jail or the grave for this hotel that ain't worth a hair of your head, or your baby daughter's, to get. Hook a fine young man and get married."

She shaped a smug smile. "I have, and I am. And I'm going to own this hotel, Mister Sims, and live happily ever after." She turned and exited into the jaws of the ravening weather. Snowflakes spangled her indigo mane like crystal stars.

He shook his head as he watched her pull her opulent machine away into the blizzard pit of twilight. The brute machine growled through the darkening city's flashbulb neon to the highway for the Big Windy. Satin flipped on the radio to her and Malique "Pony" Jones's torch ballad, Lou Rawl's "You'll Never Find." Orgasmic waves rocked her with the expectation of Pony's bed. She snorted a blow of pure cocaine. Her hand-fashioned boot stomped the golden bomb toward Pony, the bandit scourge of black Chicago's dope dealers.

Ninety miles away in fallen dark, Malique "Pony" Jones parked his tan Mercury Marquis in a side street on Chicago's Southside. He slid his black-clad Whippet frame to the street. His huge grey eyes were slits of cold-blooded purpose as he cradled, under his arm, a sawed-off shotgun in a shopping bag. A floppy black hat was jammed down on his long skull and black silky hair. Thrilly jolts of ecstasy electrified his junkie loins.

His fancy-prancy equine stride took him a half block down the ghetto street into the dingy foyer of a tenement building. Stevie Wonder's voice and music issued faintly. Pony's gloved hands slipped a Halloween fright mask across his too-pretty face. He moved silently up the foyer stairs. He faded into hall shadows facing the front ground apartment of his prey.

For tensioned eons it seemed to him he compulsively glanced at the radium face of his wristwatch as he fidgeted impatiently waiting to snap the trap. He heard Ink Spot, Bill Kenny's romantic falsetto voice, singing, "If I Didn't Care" waft from an old 78 record on the second floor. His mother's all-time favorite he remembered.

His delicate mouth fashioned a psychotic smile as he remembered how his father hated the record, despised it because, he sneered, "It's so gutless and faggy I'll puke. Shut it off or I'll stomp the record player to pieces."

The muscle-bound cocksucker hated me too, Pony thought, as he remembered how his father caved in his ribs during sadistic roughhouse play when he was a willowy kid of ten to toughen him and "grow some muscles on that sissy body," his father had vowed. He remembered how joyous he was behind his forced camouflage of token tears to see, at last, his father's monster muscles raped and slain in the coffin by the steel mill, by his father's sucker Paul Bunyan bit in blackface for the white boss's pats on his nappy head for his slave labor.

Pony fondly patted his blue steel money minter. He thought, I wish the dead and stinking bastard could see me make more money in minutes than he could hump up in a year. I wish he could see how much more lavishly I support Mama, could see how clever and bad and tough I am, could see me, for years, take off small fortunes without taking a single fall.

He heard the whoosh, felt the icy blast of the foyer door opening. He stiffened as an elderly Western Union messenger entered the foyer with the telegram he'd sent to his mark. He inched forth as the messenger drummed his knuckles against the door. His plunder lust, his buried passion for death, erected him as he caressed the shotgun crutch for his invalid ego, for the crushed image of his manhood.

Rapture barraged him to see his gargantuan shadow stalk the wall. He felt like an implacable Colossus of conquest, more ferocious than Genghis Khan. He smiled as he crowned himself Pony, the Rex of Heist! He cat-footed closer to the door of the treasure house. He remembered a late, late TV football movie line: "One for the

Gipper." He paraphrased a limerick to himself with perverse glee: One more for Satin and me and Mama makes three.

Behind the door in the living room, ebonic fatso Frank "Jelly Drop" Watson went rigid in his chair at the knock of an unscheduled caller. His mouth and nose were covered with a surgical mask to prevent inhalation of the white pile of doom dust on a card table he was packaging for his large retail trade.

He waddled to the door, peered through the dot of a peephole. "Whatta you want?" he said.

"Telegram for Mister Watson," the messenger answered.

"Shove it under the door, Pops," Jelly Drop bellowed.

"Can't; need your signature," the messenger said firmly.

"Oh shit!" Jelly Drop exclaimed as he ripped off the mask and cracked the door on the chain. He took the signature board and scribbled his name.

Pony exploded from the shadows, seized the messenger as he raised the sole of a heavy boot, kicked and crashed the chain from its moorings. Jelly Drop tumbled to his back on the carpet. Pony shoved the messenger atop him and stormed into the room. He leaned and leveled the shotgun down on Jelly Drop's head.

He commanded, "Both of you get up and sit on that couch with your hands on your head."

They trembled to their feet. The messenger scrambled to the couch. He clasped his hands on the top of his head. His false teeth chattered. Pony patted Jelly Drop's pajamas and robe before he goosed him toward the sofa with the snub barrel of the shotgun.

Jelly Drop stumbled to the couch. He collapsed on it. His hands shook on his bald head. He glared as Pony scooped up his precious merchandise into the plastic cover on the card table and shoved it into the shopping bag.

Pony's eyes were serpent bright with menace as he snarled, "Fat ass, if you blink your eyes I'll blow your head into your lap."

Pony watched the pair in a dresser mirror as he rummaged for

Jelly Drop's cash stash. He found it beneath shirts in a drawer where his junkie finger man had said it was. He backed out the shattered door into the hallway, shotgun aimed at the couch. He sprinted for the foyer door.

Jelly Drop lunged from the couch to the card table. He ripped a taped pistol from its underside. He hastened to his front window and opened it. He emptied his pistol at Pony's figure streaking down the sidewalk. The messenger fled the scene on rubbery legs. Jelly Drop smiled meager satisfaction to see Pony stumble a bit and grab at his shoulder before he disappeared into the night.

Jelly Drop's jaws were inflated with his moniker candy as he put through a coded call to his wholesaler, Razzle Red, to arrange credit purchase of a replacement batch of doom dust and to report that the phantom bandit, with Red's twenty grand price on his head, had scored again.

Satin fell into depression, felt despicably corrupt and worthless as she cruised the El Dorado down a business street on Chicago's black Southside—the street where Razzle Red turned her out on, where, for a year, she humped and frenched off myriad multiethnic johns. But she opened up Red's nose as none of his whores ever had, she told herself. She grinned lasciviously. My pussy hooked his nose tougher than the crystal blow he pigs up, she thought.

For an upper, she remembered how she got in the wind to whip her master plan on Red that recovered the piles of bread she'd humped into his pockets. She remembered how she made him find her, crawl, beg her back on her terms. "No more trick-flipping, Red; set me up in a boutique or get out of my face," she'd told him.

"I'm really something else, a helluva lady," she reassured herself. Then a downer snared her: "I've been delivering Red's dope, risking my ass for a month. Gotta cut Red and his dope loose. Soon!"

She coasted the machine into the gleaming reflection in the window of her barred boutique flashing SATIN'S in blazing turquoise neon on its gold-flecked black marble facade. She parked and went to the window to feast her eyes on the darkened elegant interior of her independence. She was appalled at how old and decadent the tear-marred makeup made her face appear in the white-lighted mirror of a jewelry display.

She thought of Pony as she used tissues and lotion from her bag to scrub her face clean. She applied fresh lipstick—Eros Scarlet. She got into the car and floated in it on steamy clouds of passion through the night toward Pony's loving.

At Sixty-third Street and Cottage Grove Avenue, she slowed the car beside an alley mouth crowded with gawkers. An ambulance squealed behind her. The crowd scrambled to the sidewalk as the ambulance turned into the alley. Satin got a flash view of a nude female child lying lifelessly in the filthy snow. In minutes, the ambulance pulled to the street and moved casually away without siren.

Shocked, Satin left her car and asked an elderly spectator, "What happened to that little girl?"

The oldster shook his gray head. "Pore chile, no more'n twelve. A dope fiend! A overdose kilt her. Guess her chums or the heartless bastid that sold her the dope dumped her like a poison dog."

Satin said, "I . . . uh . . . didn't realize kids that young shot up . . . died."

The oldster grunted, "Shoot, just last week they found a lad younger than that girl dead and stiff in a vacant house in my block . . . been so many of 'em they don't even make the papers no more."

She saw a vision of the wee girl's corpse with its only clothing a pert polka-dot ribbon in its hair, the blued discoloration of its pathetic underdeveloped breasts and bald pubic mound. She shuddered with the thought that perhaps the dope that killed the child was Red's dope, dope that she had delivered!

Satin went back to her car. As she drove away, her head vibrated with concern. "That child was just a few years older than Mimi! My God! Just a few years older than my baby!"

Satin pulled her machine to the curb in front of the Jones's neat beige stucco house in the Woodlawn District of the mid-Southside, got out, saw the flutter of living room drapes, then tread a squishy carpet of snow to the front door that opened. She rushed into Pony's arms. They kissed and clung.

"Pony, I'm so glad I didn't take you. It was so sad," she whispered.

Pony squeezed her close. "I was feeling for you, baby."

He shut the door. Arm-in-arm they went down a hallway toward his bedroom. They paused at Pony's mother's open bedroom door. They looked lovingly at the porcelain-hued, pink-gowned, delicately featured, once-beauteous belle, propped up in her canopied bed, her long fingers furiously knitting a colorful sweater for Pony. Her silky silver tresses lashed her shoulders as she cocked her head, birdlike, in that alerted way of the blind. Her unfocused hazel eyes glowed.

"Muh, dear, Etta's here," Pony said as they moved to her bed.

"Hi, Mama Lula," Satin said as she kissed and embraced the old woman.

She sighed. "Bless your darling heart, Etta, you're here. Now Malique can stop walking the house like a ghost with a toothache."

They all laughed as Pony led Satin from the room into his bedroom. They stood in the blue-lit lair deep tonguing and swaying in each other's arms with Lou Rawl's muted "You'll Never Find" creaming from the record player. They disengaged to remove her coat and boots. She sank down on the side of bed and thought she saw an odd bulge beneath the blue silk shoulder ridge of his robe as he went to the closet. Her eyes widened when he turned, with a shining face, from the closet holding a submachine gun. He tossed it on the bed beside her. She recoiled, stared at it.

He laughed. "Can't bite! Meet my bad backup buddy when I take off Razzle Red." He snapped his fingers and returned to the closet, brought back Jelly Drop's dope and money wrapped in the square of oilcloth. He dumped it into her lap, bowed grandiloquently before her.

His enormous grey eyes twinkled. "Taxes, my Queen, for our beer town dream. I collected it from Lord Jelly Drop in the province of Dopeville at Forty-seventh and Calumet Avenue."

He sat on the bed beside her and unloosened the oilcloth. The mound of "H" gleamed whitely as he plucked off its top the fat stack of greenery. He riffled it before her eyes as he exclaimed, "Five grand! . . . for two minutes of fun. And that smack I'll drop on my man in Gary for another two grand."

She stared down at the heroin, saw the OD'd child junkie again, and thought of Mimi. Then she heaved a heavy sigh.

He put his palm against her forehead. "Beautiful, you all right? That's a nice dust score!" He nibbled at her ear, her lips.

She turned her head away and slowly rolled up the oilcloth. She kissed him, looked into his eyes. "Pony, the bread is mellow, but the smack goes down the crapper." Then she stood clutching the oilcloth and walked resolutely toward the bathroom on the other side of the room.

He hollered, "Hey!" as he leapt in pursuit. He grabbed her waist and spun her to face him. His voice was harsh as he gripped her shoulders. "Have you flipped out? I stuck my head up the devil's asshole for that smack. Now come to yourself, doll. Shit!"

She stared implacably into his outraged eyes. "You know I love you, Pony, don't you?"

He nodded.

She bit her lip. "Well, Pony, guess you've got a big decision to make . . . me or this package of poison. We don't want, can't afford, the Karma dues for this shit. Darling, I hope you choose me."

He was slack-jawed, utterly flabbergasted, trapped in the indecipherable quicksand of her female temperament. He shivered his head. "You serious, baby?"

She whispered, "I'm serious, Pony."

He released her and shrugged. "I choose you, Witch. I can't make love to that smack."

She tiptoed and sucked his lips as her tender hand invaded his pajama fly to caress his weapon. Then she turned and said over her shoulder, "But you gotta do me, you gorgeous knight with the ice cream cone dick. I'll run through the shower."

He shook his head ruefully as he watched her dump the "H" from the oilcloth into the john and flush it away. After that, she stepped into the shower. He stripped himself nude. His sleek muscles rippled beneath his tawny skin like those of a jungle cat. He stretched his steel wire frame on the bed and snorted a blow of coke, and lit up a stick of gangster. He closed his eyes and drifted into fantasy about Satin and a new caper with his tongue he'd lay on her.

She slid in beside him, took the joint, and sucked on it. He held his gold snorting spoon beneath her nostrils for a heady blow. She caressed his face, his throat with fingertips. He flinched. She sat upright as she touched the bandage on his right shoulder ridge. She flipped on a nightstand light and asked, "How did that happen?"

He grinned. "Jelly Drop stung me lightly. Now don't get uptight; it's just a crease."

She gravely studied his wounded shoulder, imagined the bullet fatally hitting inches left through his throat, perhaps left and inches higher through the back of his head. She collapsed into his arms. The kiss of death kid, that's me, she told herself. She heard blind Lula flush the toilet in the hall and ground herself close to Pony. She decided she couldn't let Pony go against Red, his killer partner, Frog, and the trio of deadly New York dope dealers. The hotel dream is called off because of love, she thought. Lula and me can't make it without Pony.

Childishly she visualized Mister Sims's hotel flapping mammoth wings over the horizon like the winged greenbacks and sacks of loot in newspaper comic strips and cartoons. She whispered against his chest, "Pony, the big score is cancelled. I can't let you take the risk. We'll have to forget our Milwaukee dream."

He pushed her away, frowned as he stared into her face incredulously. "Satin, what the fuck is happening with you?"

She said, "I love you," as she swung her legs off the bed to sit on the side of it. She got cigarettes and the broker's letter from her purse on the floor. She lit two cigarettes, stuck one in Pony's mouth, and gave him the letter. She drew deeply on her cigarette.

As he read the letter, she said, "We'll have to be patient. We'll find another spot in Milwaukee to make the scum jibs swallow their poison. You won't come back against five streetwise niggers, even with a machine gun."

Pony flung the letter into her lap. He leapt from the bed, stalked the carpet before her as he furiously puffed the cigarette. Then he savagely ground it out in a nightstand ashtray. He knelt between her legs and vised her face between his palms.

Their eyes were locked as he brutally intoned, "You doubt me. You don't love me. You don't believe I'm clever enough or tough enough to take those niggers off. You maybe think Red is more man than me because he's got a bunch of bulgy muscles."

He seized her shoulders and shook her violently. "Say it! Run it down, baby! Say it! Say you think I'll freeze like a pussy and let those gorillas blow me away. Now you got a choice. Get me the dup twister to the joint where the deal goes down. We've waited three months for Red to make a deal this big. It was your idea. You got me high on it. We've got to take it off. You can't junk it, baby! I don't want you for my woman, Etta, if you don't love me enough to have confidence in me."

She understood his twisted macho reasoning as she studied his face, realized he meant it. Trapped, she burst into tears. Triumphant, he covered her face, her breasts, and thighs with kisses. Conquered, she set the alarm clock on the nightstand. She sank back on the bed. She moaned as he mounted her and stroked into her with amazing grace and equine power for an hour. He banged her womb-gate until their last mutual orgasm. Delicious fatigue dropped them into slumber. He slept between her thighs with his vanquished monster jailed inside her lubricious cave.

The jangle of the clock's alarm awakened them at dawn. They kissed and hugged. She sponged off and dressed as he watched her from the bed. She sat on the side of the bed and ran her fingers through his hair.

She said, "I'll get the meet motel key duplicated. I'll get it to you tomorrow." She lit a cigarette. She continued softly, "I think it looks great for this week. Red always rents his meet room a week before. He's checked in, as always, with luggage like a traveling salesman. So I should, within the next three days, know when Red and Frog get the call from the New York dealers, unless they call to reset the meet. It can happen. If it does, our dream is down the drain by default. Stay close and keep your phone open the rest of the week. Pony, I'm so excited. I'm going to be a wreck, darling, until it's over. I hope it comes off this week and nothing happens to you."

He said, "Nothing can. I've never made a Karma debt. I've never put the heist on or hurt an honest man."

They kissed. She stood and gazed at him for a long moment. He followed her to the front door.

He said, "Beautiful, nothing will happen to me. But I been worrying about Red and Frog hunting us down. Shouldn't I . . . ?"

She shook her head. "They don't trust each other. Frog is paranoid; he trusts nobody. It shouldn't be hard to come up with a plan to make Frog eliminate Red for us. You know how I hate Red, but it's better for us that Frog hits him. We'll worry about Frog later."

He said, "I'll pass up the smack when I take 'em off."

She said, "Oh no, you don't. Take it so we can put it out of circulation."

He groaned. "A hundred gees worth of smack down the crapper."

They laughed and kissed good-bye. He watched her pull away and disappear behind a lazy curtain of snowflakes. Twenty minutes later, she turned into the driveway through the open steel gates of Red's high-walled estate on the extreme Southside. She pressed the button on the Genie garage door opener as she drove down the long driveway into the four-car garage. When she shut off the motor, she noticed Frog's Buick, and saw that Red's Continental was missing. She stepped from the car to the driveway and pressed a button beside the garage door. It swung shut.

She glanced up at the five-bedroom apartment atop the garage where Red's stable of five whores lived. She walked to the back door of the two-story white brick mansion that was cleaned and maintained by Red's whores. She let herself into the service porch, then through the door into the gleaming spacious kitchen. She went through the lavish Chippendale dining room to the spiral staircase leading to the master bedroom.

She reached the second-floor landing, paused outside Frog's room at what she thought was the sound of her own voice. It was her voice, she realized, as she heard tinny segments of a telephone conversation she had with her shop's perfume supplier two days before. She hastened away to examine her phone, then heard Frog's door open behind her.

She halted, turned, and said frostily, "Good morning, Frog."

A frown hedge rowed his brow for an instant before he said, "Hi, Miss Fine. Didn't expect you until tonight," as he walked toward her looking like a huge black, wet frog with his protrusive eyes glittery in his blunt face, shining greasily.

She said, "Frog, the plans of mice and et cetera . . ."

He walked to her and towered over her with his heavy lips pulled back in a gold-toothed smile. "My sympathy for your mother's passing."

She said, "Thank you, Frog," as she turned away.

He grabbed her wrist. She faced him with narrowed eyes staring down at his grip on her arm. He leaned into her face with his ugly face twisted with grotesque ardor. His squeaky voice quavered. "I missed you, L'il Fox, more than Red, you can bet. Give me a break, huh? I can keep a secret."

He dropped his mouth toward hers. She jerked her face out of range and twisted her wrist from his grasp as she backed down the hallway.

He pursued and pleaded, "Gimme a break! I don't want something for nothing." He snatched a roll of "C" notes from his pocket. They littered the hallway when he threw them at her retreating feet.

She backed into her bedroom, slammed, and locked the door. Frog muttered obscenities as he got on his hands and knees to retrieve the "C" notes from the carpet. Satin hung her coat on the doorknob over the keyhole. She used a nail file to unscrew the base of the telephone. Just as she had suspected, she saw a tiny concealed transmitter bug. She replaced the screws and nervously chain-smoked at the window overlooking the backyard.

She wondered if Frog's bug was in two weeks ago; that day, the only time, she had called Pony from the house in months. And only then because she had a bad cold and didn't go into the shop for a whole day. She tried to remember the texture and text of the call. Just light chitchat she thought.

She watched Frog, in coveralls, open the garage door. He lifted the hood of his antique '38 Buick Limited, then opened a toolbox and tinkered under the hood. She left the room to check out the phones in the adjoining guest rooms. Bugged. She stopped at Frog's door, twisted the doorknob. Locked. She checked out the three phones downstairs. Bugged.

She returned to the bedroom window. She saw Red's Continental pull into the garage. He got out with his stable of wilted young whores that he had picked up off the street and from second-rate hotels in the Loop. He pecked their cheeks in turn as they went up the stairs to their pad over the garage.

Satin went into the bedroom. She stripped nude and examined her haggard face in the bathroom mirror. She heard him enter the bedroom, saw his muscular image come to stand in the doorway behind her.

He grinned crookedly as he said, "Damn, girl, you look tore down, like you been turning a slew of two-buck Spic berry pickers."

Her face was stony as she looked into his hooded green eyes in the mirror. His processed red mop glinted in the light.

"My mama had a funeral, Red. I gotta be uptight if I'm human."

He stepped in close and rubbed his crotch against her buttocks. "Aw! C'mon now, baby, with that shuck. We got in common we hate our old ladies. Right?"

She moved to brush her teeth at the side of the washbasin. "Wrong, Red! I just hated Mama's strictness, fool that I was, but I loved Mama. She didn't dump me in an alley as yours did when I was born. She wanted me, took care of me, Ora, and my pa dying of cancer. She was a saint, Red. An old church doxie cracked I was cursed for killing Mama. But she was mistaken."

She cringed away from his hands reaching for her shoulder. He laughed. "They say a trick killed my old lady. But shit, you're in serious trouble, sugar, for sure, wasting a saint."

Her dark eyes were killer panther orbs as she indicted him. "You mean you're in trouble, bad trouble, Red. You're the louse that pulled me away to break her heart with your con air castles. You murdered my sweet saint, Red! Don't you want to change the subject?"

He half-whispered, "I will, Chippie Slickstuff. Second-Story Jack swears he spotted you lollygagging around your store around midnight last night. A pure-in-heart bottom bitch don't slip back in town and detour her man's lonely bed overnight."

Contempt curled her frothy lips as she rinsed her mouth and spit into the face bowl. "Hah! I wish I had a tape to play that square-ass lonely bed crack from Razzle Red to all the jive mack men that think your swipe is frozen numb. Razzle Red, the coldest ass kicker in town. Hah! Red, you're a clown if you'll buy anything a junkie burglar tells you about your woman. Maybe you should cut me loose."

His jaw muscles writhed. He sprayed spittle. "Uh-huh! You got yourself some splitting power, you got that shop I set you up in. Now you're ready to hit the wind, to set me up as a chump laughing-stock. Right? Ha!"

She stared up at him, aquiver with the struggle to be cool. "You're wrong, Red. I don't plan to hit the wind unless you can't trust me. And, Red, please call me Etta or Satin, okay?"

He put his giant palms on the face bowl and leaned his flat yellow brute face into hers. "I couldn't get you all night at your sister's house. Why?"

She jerked her head to flounce her hair in irritation. "DA, the phone was off the hook. The calls after the funeral drove us up the wall. Can you believe, understand that, Red? Now get out of my ass, okay? I gotta headache."

He said, "How's Mimi?"

She stared in outraged awe. "None of your damned business, Red! She'd be with me if you cared." She stepped into the shower and flipped on a torrent. She lathered herself. Red's face was hideous with suspicion and rage as he glared at her soapy curves through the frosted shower door. His maximal erection tented his trousers as he peered over the shower door.

He shouted above the thunder of the water, "Ho, you got some stud's stink on you? You fucking around I'm gonna send that sucker to the morgue when I get hip to who he is. Then guess what I'm gonna do for you?"

She hollered, "Braid steel coat hangers and beat me bloody like you did when you copped me."

He screamed above the water roar, "I'm gonna have your shop torched and put you back to humping in the street where you belong."

She shouted, "Don't shuck me, Nigger. The torch I believe. But you won't share this mojo pussy, Red. And you know I'm hip. I'm the only one you can trust to deliver your dope after Smiley burned you for that bundle of bread last month. If you torch my joint, I'll cut you loose, Red."

Red busted a cobweb into the shower door with his fist. "Bitch, you ain't no precious necessity to a player. A star!"

Out of control with hatred, she shrilled, "Trick! The stupid hoes you claim are just a front for your star dope-dealing ass. Now, kick my ass. Nigger, I don't want to sell your dope! Fire me, player!"

Red stomped into the bedroom and started to undress. She finished showering and stepped out. She cut murderous eyes at Red on the bed, snorting cocaine and stroking his organ. She slammed the bathroom door, saturated a sanitary pad with mercurochrome. She belted it on around her hips to turn off Red's humping yen and ravenous tongue. She slipped into her gown.

A realization hit her. She was playing her hand stupidly with Red, waking him up with her bared hatred. She ripped off the sanitary belt and slipped off the gown. She must endure Red one more time. She relaxed her tight face in the mirror, made it bland, then sultry. After that, she opened the door and stepped sensuously into the plush pit to put Red back to temporary sleep until she could arrange his permanent slumber.

That same evening, three brothers from New York drove in and checked themselves and Red's expected kilos of "H" into a top-floor suite in a high-rise hotel. The hotel was on the extreme Southside, at the end of Red's block on the other side of the boulevard. Corpulent Mel "Ox" Hilson, the eldest, sat in the flashy suite on the living-room couch in red satin pajamas with the phone receiver to his ear. His thin, hard-faced brothers, in pink-striped dressing gowns, flanked him on the couch as they watched and listened intently.

"No, I tell you I can't deliver those shirts tonight. My sewing machine broke down. Yeah, maybe some time tomorrow. Talk to you, Red."

Mel's tar-black face was angry as he slammed down the receiver. He drummed fingertips on the coffee table before him. He lit a cigar and grunted, "That asshole has a new partner that demands to be with the transaction."

The unspoken question sparked the room like electricity as the brothers stared at one another: Is Red's new partner a narc or an informer?

Mel said, "Silas, get to the window with your binoculars. See if he is alone when he leaves the contact phone in the drugstore at the other end of the block."

Silas got the spyglasses off the coffee table and went to the window.

Jeff, the youngest brother, said, "I don't like it, Mel."

Silas returned from the window and said, "He was alone. Mel, does Red know where we're stopping?"

"Hell, no!" Mel said as he dialed the phone. "Has he ever?"

Mel said, "How ya doing, Eli? Yeah, I'm in town, gonna hoist a few with you before I leave. Listen, you ever hear of a Jake 'Frog' Stone? Fine! Give me a full rundown on him." Mel frowned, clucked, shook his head for five minutes before he said, "Eli, thanks. I love ya," and hung up with a dour face. Mel sighed. "Red's partner is an ex-burglary squad detective at Eleventh Street, Central Headquarters."

His brothers chorused, "Let's get back to the Apple."

Mel slashed a double-jointed arm through the air. "Don't panic, girls. True, since he's an ex-cop, Frog is gotta be a card-carrying snake. He got bounced off the force six years ago. He caught a five-year bit in Joliet for fencing jewelry and furs he ripped off from junkie burglars. He went to bat for wasting three of 'em, but he beat those raps."

The frozen fireworks on his giant fingers exploded dazzling light as Mel poured himself a glass of champagne. He sipped and leaned his bulk back on the couch. He grinned at his brothers. "Now, students, listen while I give you a lesson in business economics. We lugged a ticket to the joint from the Apple because the top bread in the East was fifty grand for the kilos. There's a dope panic in Chicago. So Red and his snake partner are 'coming' in their drawers to buy at a hundred grand."

Mel put a cigar in his mouth and nodded toward a lighter at the end of the table. Silas picked it up, leaned in, and flicked flame to the end of the cigar. Mel blew a blue gust of smoke toward the crystal chandelier and patted his processed gray hair.

He said, "Only a moron would lug those sizzling kilos back to the Apple to a fifty-grand market. I want you both to rent a couple of Fords or Chevys. I want Red and Frog tailed every one of their waking hours until we turn our deal. I want Red's meet spot cased before we show. I'll know where when I call him at the drugstore phone at ten in the morning.

"Well, get the hell out of here and cop those cars. Don't carry your pieces until we deal."

The brothers went into one of the bedrooms to dress. Mel went to the window to zero in with the powerful binoculars on Red's estate across the way. He said to himself, "Red's main bitch is a superfox."

Satin, resplendent in a sable-trimmed pink leather walking suit with matching boots, strolled through the front gate to the boulevard. She moved under the horny scrutiny of Mel the "Ox." Minutes earlier, Red had loaded his gaggle of whores into his Continental and left to take them to their all-night humping gigs. Mel watched her cross the boulevard and enter the drugstore. Satin went to a public phone to call Pony. She arranged to meet him on an El train platform within the hour to give him the duplicate key to Red's meet motel room on the southern outskirts of the city.

As she left the store a creative thrill shot through her: the plan to eliminate Red! She caught a cab at a stand in front of the drugstore under Mel's leering view. A quarter-hour later she paid a fare at an El station window on Fifty-eighth Street and walked up the stairway to the crowded southbound platform. Pony stood at the end of the platform, looking down on the wind-whipped street at pedestrians slogging through dirty, mushy snow. She walked to his side and looked down on the street, awash in neon.

She banged his hip with hers. "I've missed you. I love you," she whispered.

"Me you, too, Lover Doll," he said.

She slipped the dupe key into the pocket of his tan cashmere overcoat and said, "I'll call you in the morning and let you know the approximate time Red and Frog will leave to make their deal. I could almost kiss Frog."

He frowned and took his eyes from the street and stared at the side of her face. "You could what?" he growled.

She hip-banged him again and smiled wickedly. "Easy 'Ice Cream Cone.' Frog has transmitter bugs on all the phones at home. He's got a fresh lock on his bedroom door. So, he's gotta have his receiving and recording gizmos behind that door."

She paused to light cigarettes for them. "Pony, Frog's bugs gives us the way to put Red where the devil can hug him, and dogs can't bite him, as Mama used to say. Listen carefully, darling; call Red at home at one A.M. I'll pack my nicer things in the car trunk and split before you call. Baby, hang up after you say, 'Red, I've got bad news. I'm not splitting the motel score with you. I'm calling you from out-of-town. You were a dirty nigger, Red, to burn me like you did last year when we took those Dagos in Cicero. Dixie hipped me, Red, the week before his ho wasted him.'"

The Jackson Park El train pulled in to stop at the platform. They risked a kiss.

Pony said, "Damn! You're a smart broad to be so pretty."

Satin turned and dashed into the train. She blew a kiss as it pulled away to the far Southside.

Next day at twilight, Pony drove a stolen blue Pontiac in search of a highway motel sign several miles past the city limits. Ironically, he passed the two Hilson brothers on their way back to the city after casing the motel.

He spotted the sign and pulled off the highway through a thick stand of trees into the snow-choked driveway. Ten blood-red stucco units huddled, battered in a trench of snow like slaughtered soldiers dead in the hush as requiem snow blossoms fell. A Cyclops bulb winked above a blistered metal sign: OTTO'S AND GRETA'S BERLIN MOTEL. Below it, a pasteboard For Sale sign.

He parked near the office and got out with an overnight bag. His black leather jacket and cap shone under the bald eye of the sign as he went into the dimly lit office and punched a bell on the scabrous counter. He heard an ancient throat expectorate phlegm and the sound of weary feet drag toward him from a burlap-curtained rear room. An old white man in a tattered plaid robe with a matching tasseled nightcap perched on his grizzled head entered the office. He yawned sleepily.

"Welcome to the Berlin Motel, mister. Five a day, twenty by the week," he said with a heavy German accent.

Pony said, "Just overnight."

Otto smiled toothlessly as he shoved the registration pad toward Pony, blank except for Red's entry as Frank Smith, registered in room ten.

As Pony signed Leo Franklin, he said, "A friend said number nine is nice. Could business be slow enough so I got a choice?"

Otto said, "It's terrible. I'm selling. This place could be a mint again, dolled up." He sighed, "I'd dress her up pretty again if I had my Greta and a thimble of youth left." He looked at the signature, took a key from a rack, and shoved it across the counter. "Number nine you got, Mister Franklin." he said as he inked in "nine" beside Pony's pseudonym.

Pony slid a five spot across the counter, picked up his key, and went to the Pontiac. He drove it to the end of the building and sat for several minutes watching the office door. Then he took his blanket-wrapped machine gun and bag into his room, flipped the light on, and placed them under the brass bed. He went and keyed himself into adjoining number ten. He flipped on a dim nightlight and examined the large one room and bath. He decided he'd get the drop on them from the closet, in a group or however they showed.

He started to leave, turned back, and went to a tall rectangular electric heater in the wall that he thought was in the same position as his room's heater. He peered around the edges of the heater and smiled as he spotted a pinpoint of light from his room. He used a pocketknife to loosen the screws that anchored the heater's light metal housing to the wall. Then he wrenched it gently from the top. It fell loose into his hands. He pressed it and the screws back against the wall, flipped off the nightlight, left, and locked the door.

He got into the Pontiac and drove it behind an abandoned service station a hundred yards down the highway. He walked back to the motel and went behind the office building and cut the telephone line. He went into his room and locked it. He felt a draft and went into the bathroom to swing a large hinged window shut. He repeated the loosening process on his wall heater, then he pulled it off and leaned it against the gaping hole in the wall.

He glanced at his wristwatch, then pulled the suitcase from beneath the bed and took from it five sets of opened handcuffs, a coil of baling wire, five strips of double cloth sewn together with rubber balls inserted into the hollow to the middle and wire clippers. He hung the articles on key hooks affixed to his belt. After that, he blackened his room, lit a cigarette, and pulled up a chair to the window. He slit a tiny hole in the drawn drapes. For an hour and a half he smoked and peered radiant eyes through it at the access road leading to the motel.

He leaped to his feet when he saw the headlamps of Red's Continental flare on the access road to the motel. He took the machine gun to the hole in the wall and stooped in the darkness to peer through a tiny crack between the loosened heater and the wall on the other side. He heard the Continental purr into the parking lot in front of number ten and saw the headlights bomb the interior for a moment before they extinguished. Then he heard the rasp of a key.

A tall, black, overcoated shape opened the door and punched the light switch on the wall at the door. Red stood at the open door for a long moment, sweeping his eyes about the room. Pony watched him step into the room out of eyeshot and heard him open the closet door. Pony went to the drape slit and saw Frog sitting on the front seat of the Continental.

He heard Red say, "It's all right, Frog."

Pony saw Frog leave the car, carrying the pay-off valise and walk toward number ten. He heard the door shut. Pony took his fright mask from his jacket pocket, slipped it on, and went back to peer into number ten. He saw Red go to look through the parted front-window drapes for a moment before he flopped down on a sofa beside Frog, hunched inside his sheepskin coat as he clutched the valise. He watched Frog lay the valise on the sofa. Frog removed his gloves and slipped an automatic from a shoulder holster. He shoved it between the cushions beside him.

Frog said, "Red, you keep telling me those Apple niggers are on the level. But shit, I'm fifty-five and wouldn't trust Christ with my bloody fifty-grand nest egg bread, the only stick I got to fight with in this cold cruel world." Frog picked up the valise and clasped it against his chest.

Red shrugged. "I ain't got no complaints about precautions." Red rose, glanced at his watch, and said, "They're seven minutes late. I hope nothing has hap—"

Pony kicked out the heater and catapulted into the room waggling the machine gun at the bug-eyed pair, frozen in shock.

"You niggers keep your eyes off me and get on the floor, stretched out on your bellies," Pony snarled.

They flopped to the carpet as ordered, Frog still clutching the valise.

Pony tossed two pair of handcuffs between them. He commanded, "Cop Pig, unass my bread, and handcuff the pimp's hands behind him."

Frog hesitated, threw the valise at Pony's feet, and stared balefully up at Pony as he handcuffed Red's hands.

Pony ordered, "I'm gonna blow out your windows, Pig, for kicks, if you keep pinning me. Now pimping Red, turn on your side. You, Pig, ugly ass, get on your side back to back to the cunt lapper."

Frog complied. Pony rammed the snout of the machine gun into Frog's belly as he whipped a length of baling wire around their ankles, then all the way to the waists of the pair. He leaned and handcuffed Frog's hands behind his back, then mummied the pair together with baling wire to their shoulders. He stooped and tied the rubber ball gags into their mouths. Then he dragged them by their heels to the closet, crammed them into it, and closed the door.

He scooped up the valise and went through the hole in the wall to his room and smiled his pleasure as he opened the valise and gazed at the stacks of greenbacks. He put the valise beside his bag and peered through the drape slit at the access road. He remembered Satin's apprehension about the caper and thought, The bread and two gorillas bagged, with three to go. He toyed with the idea that he should split without the "H." But immediately he realized he could blow Satin if he failed to convince her that he had passed up the "H," that he hadn't dropped it on his man in Gary.

Anyway, he thought, those New York dealers might say I heisted their "H" in the parking lot as an angle to squeeze Red and Frog for restitution since the heist was plainly an inside job. No, he'd have to take the "H" as proof and suffer to see Satin destroy the powdery treasure.

Beyond Pony's view, the Hilsons sat in a parked, rented Chevy on the entry road off the highway near the stand of trees. Mel Hilson sat on the front seat with binoculars to his eyes zeroed in on the motel.

He said, "All right, Jeff, I'm satisfied . . . up to a point."

Jeff started the car and pulled out for the motel.

Silas, on the backseat, fondled an MI6 automatic rifle. He said, "Mel, up to a point means that we all don't go in. Right?"

Mel turned his face to Silas, "You're bright and right. We're gonna park back from number ten. As you know, we've got sizzling, pre-cious merchandise. So if any bastard, except that old peckerwood land prop comes near that door, blow the hot shit out of him, cop or whoever. Stay down out of sight. Understand that, Silas? Don't fuck around thinking about it! I'll say it again, blow away any cocksucker that shows!"

Jeff tooled down the access road into a parking space, facing number ten, fifty yards away. They got out, with Mel carrying the dope satchel. They walked casually toward number ten, paused, and looked into the front and rear of Red's Continental.

Pony spied through his drape slit. He saw the top of Silas's head as he crouched on the rear floorboards. He went through the hole in the wall to stand behind the door of number ten.

Pony said, "Yeah?" at the sound of the jiggled doorknob, then the knock on the door.

Mel said, "Mel."

Pony stayed behind the door as he swung it open. They stepped inside. He slammed it shut and smashed the machine-gun butt down on the top of diminutive Jeff's skull. His eyes rolled as he fell forward against Mel, knocking him off balance as Mel tugged a pistol halfway out of his overcoat pocket. Pony slammed the machine-gun barrel against Mel's jaw. The brothers lay unconscious on the floor. Pony handcuffed, bound, and gagged them. He dragged them by the heels into the bathroom.

He picked up Mel's satchel, checked it, and took it through the hole to his room, where he removed his mask. He grinned as he peeped at the Chevy and saw Silas's sentry head silhouetted above the front seat.

Pony went to the bathroom window. He opened it and threw machine gun, satchel, valise, and his bag through the window. He climbed out and dropped into the snow at the back of the building. Almost leisurely, he walked across a frozen field to the stolen Pontiac behind the abandoned service station. He threw his loot in and got behind the wheel and pulled out to the highway for his house on the mid-Southside.

Two hours later, Red moaned in silk shorts on his bed as Satin tenderly applied a Benzocaine cream to Red's baling wire burns and bruises sustained while thrashing on the closet floor in frantic efforts to escape before suspicious Silas came to discover the heist. Frog, in a bathrobe, sat on the side of the bed glaring down at Red's back with a combination expression of anguish, murderous rage, and suspicion.

Frog said, "Somebody fingered us. Put your thinking cap on, nigger. We got to get that dope and bread back. You heard those Hilsons swear to hit us if we don't square up with them within seventy-two hours."

Red, propped up on the pillows, groaned as he raised a platinum cocaine-snorting spoon toward his nostrils. Satin glanced at her wristwatch.

Frog slapped the spoon from his hand. He darted a suspicious look at Satin and said, "Let's go to the den, Red, now."

Red struggled up to his feet, threw a robe across his shoulders, and followed Frog to the den at the end of the hall.

Frog slammed the door behind them. Red collapsed on the sofa and peered at Frog through his fingers pressed against his face. Satin stuffed perfume bottles from the dresser into her purse.

Frog jerked a chair to the sofa. He sat down in front of Red, jabbed his kneecap with his fist, and asked in a deadly whisper, "Red, did you crack to your black bitch about where we went to deal?"

Red shook his head, "Nothing!"

Frog said, "You crack to anybody?"

Red said, "Nobody, Frog . . . Did you, Frog?"

Frog curled his lips, "I'm not stupid, nigger. That motel key, maybe that black bitch knew from that. Nigger, where did you keep that key?"

Red lied. "In my wallet, Frog. She's not hooked into that heist. For what reason would she put her man in a cross like that after I took her off the street and set her up in the boutique? Why, shit, Frog, she's living!"

But immediately Red thought of the bitter argument with Satin. He remembered her accusation that he was responsible for her mother's death.

Frog laughed contemptuously. "That was a fancy-walking young nigger that took us off, Red. I saw his wrists. He was a yellow nigger, maybe pretty. He had big, grey, ho eyes peeping through his mask. Red, you'll never meet a pitch-black ho that wouldn't suck a pretty young yellow nigger's shit through a straw. You ain't pretty no more, Red, and you're old at forty-five to a young ho twenty-two. You conned, gorillaed that bitch, coat-hangered her and turned her out. Red, don't bullshit yourself that she wants or needs you. I say let's stomp that bitch and find out who cut that caper. I'm a police scientist, and I'm sure she's the finger."

Red groaned and pressed his palms against his temples. "You're wrong, Frog . . . You're wrong."

The phone rang on an end table beside Red. He picked up. His mouth sagged open as he listened to Pony's strange voice reciting a conundrum. He ashened and sputtered, "Wha . . . uh . . . who . . . uh?" Red's hand shook as he replaced the receiver. He stared into Frog's cold eyes.

Frog leaned into Red's face. "Who was that, Red?"

Red averted his eyes and mumbled, "Some mush-jib Polack dialed the wrong number, that's all . . . Christ Almighty! You ain't leery of me, are you, Frog?"

Frog rose to his feet and patted Red's shoulder. He smiled. "Hell, no! Everything is gonna be all right, partner. I got an idea I'll lay on you when I get back from the john."

Frog opened the den door and stepped into the hallway to collide with Satin, dressed for the street. He seized her around the waist under the guise of support and grinned down into her face, "Baby doll, it's after one. Ain't you afraid you'll get ripped off for that mink benny lollygagging in them streets?"

She managed to say smoothly, "Yes, I would, lollygagging. I've got a yen for barbecued ribs. Want me to bring you an order?"

He released her. "Bring me a fifth of Cutty Sark. I'll give you the bread when you get back."

Satin stuck her head inside the den. She smiled at Red. "Want anything from the street, sweetheart?" she asked Red, slumped on the sofa.

He stared at her for a long moment before he said, "Pall Malls, Satin, if you're coming back . . . soon."

She said, "I'll bring them back, Daddy . . . soon." She exhaled tension as she went down the hall toward the stairway.

Behind his door, Frog sat on the side of his bed loading bullets into his six-shot, thirty-two revolver. He put a silencer on the barrel as he listened to Pony's tape-recorded voice.

Satin drove her El Dorado down the mansion's driveway into boulevard traffic. Silas Hilson was staked out on the boulevard behind her in a rented Chevy. He reflexively started the car to tail her, but he turned the engine off as he remembered that Mel instructed him to tail only Red and Frog.

A half-dozen miles away, Pony dressed for the street to get some butterscotch ice cream for his mother and champagne for a celebration with Satin before the liquor store closed.

With tape recorder in hand, handcuffs behind his back, and revolver in his robe pocket, Frog walked into the den. He drew the gun and pointed it at Red's head. "Stick out your hands, Red," he ordered.

Sweat popped on Red's brow as he held out his hands. Frog whipped the cuffs from behind his back and snapped them around Red's wrists. Red's mouth fell agape. Red stared at him as he plugged the machine into a wall socket, then set the recorder on the floor at Red's feet. Frog sat down in the chair before Red. He scooted it back a couple of feet from Red after he flipped on the recorder.

Frog pointed the revolver at Red as Pony's rapid voice said: "Red, I've got bad news. I'm not splitting the motel score with you. I'm calling you from out-of-town. You were a dirty nigger, Red, to burn me like you did last year when we took off those Dagos in Cicero. Dixie hipped me, Red, the week before his ho wasted him."

Frog leaned carefully and flipped off the machine.

Red's lips soundlessly flapped together as he pitifully extended his cuffed hands toward Frog. Finally, Red croaked out, "Frog, it's a cross!"

Frog aimed the gun at Red's heart. "Don't speak to me, Red!" he said venomously.

Red collapsed against the sofa back.

Frog mused in a deadly monotone. "A cross that backfired, Red. Now I know why you were so certain your bitch was innocent when I was so sure she was the finger. We could have cut that smack twice and made a ton of bread in the panic. Your greed, Red, is gonna put a tag on your toe. I'm an old, ugly nigger . . . broke! 'Frog Mug' the kids in the orphanage called me, the funny face that nobody adopted . . . loved . . . never had any pussy I didn't buy. I was guilty of those three murders I beat, but you'll never tell it, Red. Shot Marva first . . . told me she was cutting me loose, told me she retched when I made love to her. After all the dope I bought her, clothes, paid rent for her junkie brother and her Q.T. sweetie. I killed them all shooting up dope I bought. I was sorry I killed her . . . still am. Ain't that a bitch, Red? My nose is still open for that yellow, stinking, skunk, lousy, junkie ho. You can speak now, Red. Tell me the name of that bandit so I . . . uh . . . we can trace him and recover that money and dope."

Red's eyes sparkled with fear and cunning as he said, "Frog, you were right about Satin. I lied about the key to cover that I was stupid enough to trust her. The key was on the dresser all the time. Uncuff me, Frog, and we'll stomp the name of the bandit out of her. Frog, the description fits the bastard that took off Jelly Drop and the other dealers, even the prancy walk. Don't make a mistake, Frog, and waste me. You'll need me against the Hilsons until we bag the bandit."

Red saw Frog's finger tighten on the trigger as he replied, "No sale, Red. I don't need you. I can't gamble on you. Your body dumped in an alley and that recording of your bandit double-crosser clears me with the Hilsons. Why did his call shake you up, Red? Why did you lie? C'mon, Red, I'll give a condemned man a chance to con me why he lied."

Red stared stupidly at him, slack-jawed, a portrait of guilt as he flogged his brain for the logical words to explain why he lied. He tensed, and decided to bomb Frog's jaw with his foot. Red leaped to his feet and blurred a slippered foot toward Frog's head at the instant he saw the chambers of the revolver start to roll. His dead foot grazed Frog's head as he crashed to the floor with a leaking red hole in the center of his forehead.

Frog rose from his chair and pumped two bullets into the back of Red's head. He stared down at Red, the smoking pistol in his hand. He stripped off Red's flannel robe and wrapped it around Red's bloody head. Then he dragged the corpse into his bedroom closet. He sat on the side of the bed and thought about the problem of the body and what to do about Satin when she returned.

Satin arrived at Pony's house ten minutes after he left for Lula's ice cream and the celebration champagne. Satin stood patiently outside the front door listening to the metallic clatter as Lula unbolted and unbarred the thick oak door. She stepped into the house and helped Lula refortify the door.

Near Forty-seventh and Calumet Avenue, Jelly Drop stepped from his bathtub. He talced his blubber and slipped into fresh white silk pajamas. He scooped up a new porn mag from a living-room table. He went to the bedroom and propped himself on satin pillows in his king-size bed. He opened the mag and grinned salaciously as he started to enjoy the erotic contents. He reached a hand into a tall candy crock on the nightstand beside him. Dramatic pain creased his face as he peered into the empty crock. He swung his tree stump legs off the bed and turned the crock upside down on his palm. He licked his palm clean of the sugar crystals.

He sighed as he slipped on his overcoat over his pajamas. He put on shoes and socks and went to a drugstore around the corner on Forty-Seventh Street. He pressed his face against the door to attract the attention of clerks and cashier hustling to go home.

A porter came to the door and threw his hands in the air. "We closed, man!" he hollered before he broomed away.

Jelly Drop turned disconsolately away. He waddled to his car parked in front of his apartment building. He unlocked the car, got in, and pulled away for a sure shot source of jelly drops. Fresh! He sped down Martin Luther King Drive to Sixty-first Street. He turned and pulled up to park in front of a drugstore. Open! He got out and started across the sidewalk.

The corner of his eye snared a figure with a unique equine stride walk from a parked tan Mercury Marquis across the sidewalk into a liquor store in the middle of the block. Jelly Drop forgot his candy dope. He scuttled to the liquor store window and peered in at Pony standing at the rear of a long line of last-minute customers. Jelly Drop told himself, "He's the size, the height. It's him!" He scrambled to a drugstore phone to call Red.

Frog picked up the phone in the den on the second ring. He listened to Jelly Drop's excited report. Frog said, "Take that Marquis's registration card off the steering post. Don't try to memorize his address! Don't try to tail him. You might wake him up. Call me to give me his address as soon as you get the card. Don't mention this to anybody!" Frog hung up. He went to dress for the street.

Jelly Drop went to Pony's unlocked car and shakily got the registration card. He went back to the drugstore phone to dial Frog and read off Pony's address. Frog loaded his revolver, locked his bedroom door, and went to his Buick in the garage. He drove down the driveway to the boulevard. Frog was too excited to detect Silas Hilson pull out behind him, tail him to Pony's block. Frog parked near the corner a half block from Pony's house.

Silas parked a half block away in the next block. Pony's Marquis and Satin's El Dorado were parked in front of the Jones's house. Silas eased out to the street. He walked to a public phone in the middle of the block where he was parked and called Mel.

Inside the house, Pony and Satin giggled in a haze of dust as they slit the heavy gauge plastic-wrapped kilos of "H" with razor blades and flushed the powder down the toilet. After the last of it was flushed, they lay nude on the bed and sipped champagne. Their eyes were hooded with the narcosis of the inhalation of the "H" dust. They kissed and fell asleep with their lips and bodies locked together.

Two hours later, Frog left his Buick. Gun in fist he went to the rear of the Jones's house. A killer Doberman snarled and lunged from the shadows. He blew a hole in its head in midair with his silenced gun. He dropped his gun into his overcoat pocket. He made a hole in a basement window over the latch. He dropped into the basement. Silas, with MI6 rifle, hid in the shrubbery in the front of the house. Mel and Jeff went to the rear of the house and waited in the shadows, with guns drawn.

Frog ascended stairs to the locked door to the kitchen. He opened a pocketknife, struck a match. He shimmied the spring lock open with the knife blade. He drew his revolver. He stepped into the dark kitchen and went through it into the dimly lit hall. He stopped at the sound of Lula's snoring at the end of the hall. He moved to Pony's open bedroom door. He stepped inside and stared down at the intoxicated lovers locked together, with the valise of cash gaped open beside them. He held the gun an inch from Pony's temple and pulled the trigger. Pony jerked spastically. Pony's movement and the air-from-a-punctured-tire sound of the gun awakened Satin. She stared gigantic eyes up at Frog over his gun in her face.

Frog grinned and whispered, "High and mighty ho! I couldn't fuck you one way, so I'll fuck you the sweetest way there is." He pulled the trigger and stared at the sudden hole between her glazed open eyes.

Frog turned to search the room for the dope. He noticed the pile of plastic in the bathroom wastebasket. He stooped and saw the inside of the toilet rimmed with "H," the floor dusty with it. He fastened the valise, put it under his arm, and went to the side of Lula's bed. She stirred and stared sightlessly up at him.

"Malique, is that you?" she asked in a sleepy voice.

Frog's finger was tight on the trigger. He waved the gun before her eyes. Then he turned and went to the barred front door. He frowned at the heavily fortified door, turned, and went to the back door. He unbolted it, opened it, and peered into the shadow-haunted backyard. He stepped into the night.

The sound of Mel's and Jeff's barraging silenced pistols were like a dozen tires popping as the bullets cavorted and slammed Frog against the side of the house. He fell lifelessly to the frozen earth.

Malicious winds off Lake Michigan scattered and sailed the spill of bills from the unlatched valise.

# GRANDMA RANDY

## I

In 1938, Jay Henderson sat suspect in a klieg of Texas sun, a disheveled rodeo cowboy Apollo. Big green money lay like bouquets of wilted blossoms in front of him and at center table. He felt threatened in the breathy silence beneath a gimlet battery of bloodshot eyes. His insides queased in the rancid odors of nicotine, the emotion stink of his opponent. He felt suffocated by the sour whiskey gusts from the four busted-out hard-faces leaning in with sullen flabbergast to detect a cheat angle, or even a rational explanation of how their perennial sucker had wiped them out.

Atom-deep fatigue stained Jay's eye sockets like blue shadow makeup. But his violet eyes shone with frantic vivacity behind sunglasses as they scanned the brute face of his surviving opponent: Sol "Wildman" Starkey, rodeo star and high stakes stud poker player—and peerless hard loser.

Starkey grunted and hunched his buffalo shoulders. He pushed his tap-out pile of green into the pot. He rapped his knuckles against the table. "C'mon now, Cutie Face, call that two thou raise or pass," Starkey drawled. "Call! 'Cause I ain't got no disrespect for that ten high club flush you maybe got."

He took a hit from a whiskey bottle, then lit a trademark cigar to signal his win of the first substantial pot in almost fifty hours. The gallery leaned in closer on their chairs.

Jay stared at Starkey's apparent jack high diamond flush hand on the tabletop. He shifted his eyes to zero in on the center of Starkey's freckled forehead. In his crucial bet situation he heard, as he had for two days, whirring high voltage electrical sounds inside his skull. Then like from an echo chamber, the infallible read-out tip-off voice of his budding super-sensitized schizophrenia boomed: "Starkey's bluffing!"

Starkey ribbed, "C'mon, boy, don't just sit there eyeballing me like a possum in a tree. Play poker!"

Jay smiled as he scooped up his winning hand and shuffled it into the deck. He knew that Starkey considered himself undressed without a pistol. And worse, he remembered Starkey's penchant to use his pistol to reverse a tap-out. Yes, he told himself, unarmed as he was, it would be hazardous to his health and winnings to tap-out Starkey along with the others.

Starkey grinned extravagantly as he flipped over the black spade jack in the hole that paired the diamond jack. He pulled the pot in. He hee-hawed and winked at the gallery. "Don't you know, friends, it feels good, real good, to sock a stiff one on him?"

The gallery chuckled.

Starkey scowled as he watched Jay scoop up his bundle of green and stand. "Look here, boy, it ain't sporting to quit now. We gonna play a few more hands to give me some kinda justice," Starkey said as his hand fiddled at the butt of his pistol in his waistband.

One of the gallery piped up, "Yeah, give the man a shot to get even."

Jay shook his head as he peeled off two hundred in walking money for the four losers. He scooted fifty-buck portions to them on the tabletop. Then he stripped his yellow bandana from his throat and tied his winnings into it. His knees quivered as he walked toward Starkey's front door.

Starkey followed him and shoved his palm against the door as he opened it. "Boy, you clipped me for ten grand and the others for at least another five. I'm gonna call you in a coupla days for another go-round. You coming, ain't you?"

Jay shrugged, "Sure, why not? Nobody living can beat me playing poker. Not any more!"

Starkey removed his hand from the door. Jay stepped into the Sunday sunshine. He stood on the porch, a blinking, booted portrait of woe slumped in his wrinkled pastel-blue cowboy suit. Wisps of lank golden hair scaggled the edges of his tan ten-gallon hat as he went down the walk and got into his spanking-new 1938 white Caddie parked at the curb. He cruised away through the bustling Houston streets to the northside and Ila, his teenage inamorata.

As he parked on the tree-shaded street, an electrical fire issued smoke from beneath the hood and deadened the engine. He leapt from the car and put out the flames with a fire extinguisher from the trunk. He cursed as he slammed down the hood.

He heard a Glen Miller band recording blasting from his pink stucco bungalow accompanied by the bedlam of a Saturday night party still in riotous progress. He moved up the walkway determined to evict the familiar mob of freaked out sluts and studs.

"I'm only twenty-seven, and I feel like my own grandpa," he lamented. "You're an idiot, a star sucker to hold on to Ila," he told himself. "She's poison, a tramp. Throw her out!" But, he remembered a pathetic vision of himself humiliated, groveling when he was forced to find her, apologize, and beg her back. Once he begged, literally, on his knees as she marinated him with her sewer-mouth abuse. "I hate her, but I can't do without her," he told himself bitterly as he rammed his key in the lock and twisted himself into the shambled living room.

Remnants of his filet steaks lay on cigarette-butted plates stacked on the beer can-littered coffee table. High heels, panties, jeans, and condoms were strewn on the carpet. Dead soldiers of scotch and bourbon glittered from the wastebasket. A half-dozen nude teenaged couples, pretzeled on the couch, chairs, and floor, chattered and laughed raucously. They raised eyebrows, and then ignored him as he moved past them through a smog of hash smoke toward his bedroom.

He halted slit-eyed in the hallway and knotted his fists at the appearance of a strange, brawny, teenage jock prancing from his bedroom toward him with a con grin on his foxy face.

"Whew! Man, I'm glad you showed. I'm Freddie. You must be Jay, Ila's old man. I been helping your old lady with the party and stuff. You know, I been making like a bouncer keeping everybody from tearing your joint down and bad asses from crashing in." Lipstick smeared Freddie as he stuck out his palm.

As Jay limply slapped his palm, he noticed the lipstick indictment on his face was Passionate Scarlet. Ila's. The jock's fly gaped open, smudged red. This bastard's fly is flying her flag too, he thought. She had to French him to brand him there.

"I can't find words to thank you, Freddie, for everything," he said with a hideous smile.

Freddie gave him a fist in the arm. He gave Freddie a return shot, hard, as he went past him. Jay continued down the hall to the bedroom door. He pushed it half open.

Transfixed like a voyeur stranger, he peered through the door crack at Ila nude. She was squatting in the center of the gold-quilted bed flogging her five-inch cone of jet pubic bush with a silver brush. His weapon tingled as he gazed at her incredibly fat-lipped snare, its shocking pink gate aflash. Her hair, Betty Grable-styled, framed her pixie face like an indigo halo. "Why does she have to be so luscious and so lowlife?" he groaned mutely.

Bite and suck bruises lividly pocked her pulse-sprinting curves from epic chest to sculpted inner thighs. She has to be the most irresistible orphan that was ever born, and the most corrupt, he thought. Somehow I have to find the balls to let her go before she compels me to do something I don't ever want to do again, he told himself as he punched his door wide open with his fist.

Her grey eyes, beclouded with dope, zoomed in wide on him, rosebud lips slung loose in alarm for the instant before she recovered her sloe-eyed cool. He moved to sit on the side of the bed. She recoiled in mock disdain. He studied her with an expression of treacherous bemusement on his stubbled face as he waited for the witty overlay of her offensive defense of her tramphood.

Suddenly, she snapped her fingers, frowned in the throes of fake recall. "Now, let me see . . . you're . . . uh . . . No, don't help me. Ah! I've got it! You're that skid row pukey bum that conned me out of a buck the other day. Sure, you're the one . . . you stink the same . . . said you hadn't dirtied a plate in days. So, what the fuck you doing here in my face?" She paused to push the nitty-gritty sound out. "I didn't invite your broke ass to the party."

He hurled the bulged-with-loot bandana into her face.

She tore it loose, caressed her long, tapered fingers through the treasure, moaning carnal hype. "Ooeeee! Oh shit! Sweet Da Da, whoooo wheeeee! You do it to your baby so good." She catapulted herself toward him.

He stiff-armed her back and stood. "Don't touch me, Ila! Get on a robe and bounce your parasite pals." He jiggled his head spastically. "I can't trust myself to do it."

Cat eyes saucered and luminous, she said quietly in her whispery knife-at-his-heart way, "Your old ass I will. You reneging on our latest understanding? Remember? I do what I want with whoever I want to do it with. Are you creaming again to crap on your li'l free spirit? Huh?"

He said, "No, Ila, you got the best hand. Now." He went to the closet, extracted a carbine, and rammed in a cylinder of shells. "All right, I'll be fair and ask them one time to go away. Then, I'll blow them away," he said tremulously as he moved toward the door.

She sprang from the bed and seized him around the waist and

spun him. "Hey! You flipping out?" she exclaimed as she blocked the doorway.

He smiled sweetly. "Then, Ila, please, will you make them go away?"

She nodded frantically as she led him to the bed. He dropped the rifle to the carpet and sat down heavily on the bed. She stooped and tugged off his boots, pressed him back on the bed, and lifted his legs onto the bed. She kissed his forehead, walked to the closet, and slipped on a gauzy wrapper. She left the room and shut the door.

Dizzy with fatigue, he lit a cigarette, decided he'd have to take a short nap to energize himself a bit before undressing for a shower. He closed his eyes—then opened them wide in apprehension about his threat to blow away Ila's friends. I really wasn't serious, never out of control. Yes, I was bluffing. I was tired and angry and just bluffing, he told himself desperately. But then, he told himself, it was better after all that Ila bounced them to save me the risk of wasting the bastards.

He closed his eyes and tried to remember the details of an article on fatigue he'd read. He felt certain it could be a killer long term. His mother, Sarah, was an example victim, he thought.

His mind untethered, staggered catacombs of pain. He saw a vision of her, as vivid as the Arkansas stars in summer, lying on her deathbed in their lopsided coal miner's shack. In a storm of tears, he begged her not to leave him and his pa. He knew how much she loved them both. His seven-year-old mind just couldn't comprehend why she could be so eager, so cruel to die and desert them.

Her gasps and the doomsday thump-a-bump of her tired heart terrified him as he lay in her arms waiting for the company doctor and his pa.

"Ma, don't leave me and Pa. Ain't long I'm gonna be big and workin' the coal with Pa. Then we gonna buy you a ritzy house . . . 'lectric lights! . . . a great big slew of snazzy furniture. Ain't that somethin', Ma? And that ain't all. A john—inside! Honest, Ma! And a new magic 'lectric washtub to do all the washin' you got 'cept the throwin' in. That's what Pa and me gonna do, Ma. So please, Ma, don't leave me and Pa. We love you, Ma."

He raised his head from her bosom to see her promise not to leave. He burst into tears. She looked sixty. How could she be just thirty-two?

She smiled, closed her eyes, and sobbed, "Pa's sweet on scum, that Binnie on Red Light Hill. I ain't sorry to leave your pa. He ain't got no feelings left for me nohow since her. Forgive me for leaving you, but I'm too tired and ugly to try to stay. Anyway, I got an invite to peace and rest."

Suddenly she bolted upright, seamed face ashine, dull blue eyes fired by the glory vision of the beckoning Master Keeper of the sweetest, longest dream there is.

She clapped her hands in joy and shouted, "Hallelujah!" then lay back and died.

He wept, thrashed, and pounded the spiny pine floor in convulsions of pain until his fists were bloodied and torn by splinters. Pa never got back with the doctor, never even got to him. Whiskey and Binnie had ambushed him on the way.

He found his pa through a tear in a shade at Binnie's shack on Red Light Hill. Pa was whimpering and groveling naked, kissing and licking the feet, anus, and sex nest of Binnie, the giantess, in patent leather boots cursing and whipping him savagely with a cat-o-nines to howling climax.

He crashed their party through the shack door. Wailing, he hawked and spat on Binnie. She punched and kicked him as his pa feebly tried to restrain her. She beat and whipped them both into submission. Then wept, apologized, as she smothered them against her bosom.

Jay remembered how Binnie, the rouge-smeared schemer, got the house with the toilet hole inside from his Ma's life insurance policy payoff shortly after her cremation; how after Binnie had rinsed her dishwater blond hair to platinum and sausaged her Mae West dimensions inside peep-show dresses, she was the envy of all the two-buck pieces of meat with holes on Red Light Hill.

He thought, with a freakish ping in the scrotum, of the nine years Binnie had her sexual way with Pa and himself, exploited them like slaves. He shaped an ugly smile recalling the morning his pa cancelled his hatred when he shot out Binnie's lights.

On the screen behind his closed eyes he saw himself about to rise for his shift in the coal pits. He heard the guttural whisper of the Maserati when it coasted to a stop outside his window. He heard the tipsy bray of Binnie's voice. He went to the window, saw Casper, the elderly and notorious bisexual Lothario that had picked her up in the evening, groping Binnie in the funeral glow of dawn.

He heard his pa suffering a black lung paroxysm of coughing from his bedroom above. Then he listened to the sounds of Pa struggling from the bed that he hadn't been out of in several months, heard him stumbling across the floor to the window, to the closet, down the stairs. He cracked his door, saw gowned Pa, Magnum rifle in hand, his rotten lungs wheezing as he opened the front door.

He froze in exhilaration to see Pa brace his wasted frame against a doorjamb, aim, and put his sharpshooter eyes to the rifle sights. A minisecond before the percussive roaring, the lapping of orange tongues of flame, the couple's phosphorescent eyes locked on the rifleman. Then a gout of crimson leapt from Binnie's forehead. Casper ducked out of sight. He felt tidal waves of joy rock him to see Binnie dead. He walked toward Pa, who collapsed and wept piteously.

As he reached Pa and stooped to lift him, a muffled blast punched his eardrums. Blood and brain gore splattered him. He winced to see the end of the rifle barrel rammed into Pa's throat. He dropped to his knees and clasped his shattered dead ringer image close to his chest.

"I don't hate you no more, Pa," he sobbed. "I ain't never thought about leaving you sick. I took care of you, Pa, 'cause Ma loved you. But I ain't never gonna forgive you, Pa. Not for Ma!" he screamed through bared teeth.

He remembered how, stripped penniless by Pa's sickness and Binnie's passion for the ponies and craps, he traded the dilapidated house off to the mortician for Pa's decent burial. He thought of how he rode the rails, begged, and stole for months until lost and dazed, he circled back through a dozen states to Galveston, Texas.

Now, in his bed, he heard the rustle of taffeta interrupt his bitter reverie. The musk of a dead woman, a murdered woman startled him. He slowly opened his eyes, plastered his hands across his eyes, trembled as he stared through his fingers at the nightmarish apparition smiling wickedly at him from a chair near the door. Grandma Randy! "I must be dreaming!" he exclaimed to himself.

"You're not dreaming, kiddo," he heard the obese crone say in her unmistakable whiskey contralto.

He shuddered, knew he was dreaming. He razored red-hot rills across the back of his hand with his fingernails to discover he was awake.

She stroked gem-littered fingers across the bluebonnet blossom pinned in her red hair and primly pulled the hem of blue taffeta down across her lumpy knees as she grinned salaciously.

I'm awake. But she can't be alive, unmarked over there. She's dead. I killed her in self-defense, he argued with himself as he stared hypnotized as she took a cigarette from a jeweled case, flicked flame to the cigarette tip, inhaled. He watched her exhale, smelled the poltergeist of smoke as it floated through the air. He popped sweat. The murderess had come back from the grave as she'd warned him.

"Yes, I'm back to punish you, dearie. You fool! I told you you couldn't kill Satan's pet. Remember?"

I'll kill her again, I'll blow her away, he thought, before she kills me.

She airily waved a pudgy hand. "I'm not going to kill you, kiddo, not personally, that is. My lovelies will for that horrid thing you did to me and them with your baseball bat. Remember? Homer and Abigail are here in this house waiting to chastise you. Happy, happy, kiddo," she said as she dredged up her bulk from the chair. She threw her head back and laughed.

He darted a glance at the carpet to locate the carbine. He leaned and scooped it up. He swung it toward her to fire. She had vanished. He leapt from the bed, scrambled to fling open the door. Ila faced him. He grabbed her, darted a fearful glance back into the bedroom.

"You see a fatso old broad?" he shouted.

Ila shook her head.

"Well, don't go in the bedroom! Stay in open spaces until I search the house!" he warned.

"What the hell is happening, Ding-a-ling?" Ila asked as he seized her wrist and pulled her down the hallway to the kitchen.

"Shut up, bitch! We got guests. King cobras!" he screeched.

He snatched a flashlight from the refrigerator top. With carbine in arm, he and Ila searched every shadowed nook and cranny of the house. They went to the basement, stood at the threshold, staring at the piles of junk furniture and odds and ends that the former owner had abandoned.

He shook his head. "It's too dangerous to search this mess. We've got to get out of this house until I think of a way to find and kill those snakes," he said as he shut the basement door.

He led Ila to the bedroom to stuff his poker winnings into a leather shaving kit. After that, they went to the living room, flopped down on the sofa. His face was tortured as he mopped sweat from his brow with his sleeve.

She studied him, remembered that a boy in the orphanage was

frightened by things nobody else ever saw before he was taken away. She chewed her bottom lip as she tried to remember the medical term she'd heard that applied to the derangement.

Ila finger-stroked his temple as she said gently, "I love you, and I'm worried about you, Jay, baby. I just don't understand how that old woman that you saw could sneak in the house and out, and I never saw her. It's impossible!"

He cut hostile eyes at her. "She was here!"

"But what if she wasn't? What if it's really your . . . uh . . . nerves?" Ila said.

He batted her hand from his temple. "I'm not crazy, girl!" he snorted.

At that instant she recalled the mental derangement term. Paranoid schizophrenia! Fear narrowed her eyes as she moved away a bit.

She said, "So we've got a problem, snakes in the basement. Do we sit here and wait for them to die of old age?"

He shaped a cunning smile of triumph. "We'll check into a hotel until I can get the exterminators to put a tent over the house and gas it Monday. What kills roaches and rats will sure as hell snuff cobras," he said as he picked up the phone to call a cab.

They sat in silence waiting for the cab.

Finally she said, "The old lady? Where did you know her?"

He jerked his head to stare at her. "In Galveston. Now, Ila, dummy up about her."

They heard the honk of the cab. They left the house and went down the walk to get in.

"She won't be able to sneak into the house after I steel bar all the windows and doors," he whispered into Ila's ear as he patted her thigh.

"Jay, the old broad you thi—you saw. Who is she?" Ila pressed.

He glared at her. "Forget her! I mean it!" he said sternly.

His mind whirled madly as the cab pulled away into the peaceful and salubrious Houston twilight. At midnight, in a downtown hotel bed, wide awake, Jay clutched sleeping Ila in his arms. He remembered how the seedlings of his madness had been planted a decade before in Grandma Randy's mansion of horrors.

## II

Jay saw himself at seventeen. He vividly recalled how he had palpitated in Grandma's horror mansion at his teenage sweetie's coded knocking on his bedroom ceiling from the attic above. He rapped a softball bat against his ceiling in reply. Then he went to a furnace vent in the wall, listened for movement in Grandma's first-floor bedroom below.

"Hi, Ice Cream Cone, it's clear!" he stage-whispered into the vent. Then he made a kissy sound of cunnilingus.

"Ooeee!" a honeyed voice squealed through the attic vent.

Joyfully he flung himself back into his bed. Thumbtacked shots of rodeo superstars riding and roping studded the walls. He gazed at them, certain he'd join their ranks one day.

Shortly, Fay, a dazzling platinum-haired girl, eased into his room and flung herself onto the bed into his arms. The teenage waifs caressed and kissed ravenously, clung together in the county-accredited foster home for the first time since their arrest ten days before. His house-pet cowboy suit, pearl grey and crisp, sprawled on a chair aglow like a decapitated ghost in a laser of Texas dawn.

He tongue-flogged her navel, her inner thighs. She pulled and mauled his ears. He moaned ecstatically. They flinched, jerked apart at the flash of dormitory lights on the windowpane, followed by the clang of a wake-up bell.

He ground his face against her vulva. "Oh, no!" he groaned.

She said, "Dammit! I woke up late and blew the sugar. But first chance, Candy Dong, I'll be back to do the do."

She kissed his navel and burrowed her face and head into his crotch. Reluctantly, she stood and her bantam curves outrageously bulged her coarse cotton nightgown. Her fawn face was ethereal in the murk as she gazed at him.

She whispered, "I love you, Jay. You want me, too?"

He said, "Me you too, Fay. Who you want wasted to prove it?"

They laughed.

She bit her lip. "I've got the creepies. Can't we please put this place down soon? Like tonight?"

His handsome face twisted for an instant in irritation. "Baby, c'mon now, no bread is what got us here. But you gotta admit, it's got the Galveston juvenile slammer skunked all to hell. I hoboed to Texas," he said as he moved to sit on the side of the bed. His arms embraced her waist. "But, we're gonna ride the cushions soon as I can . . . ah . . . borrow a hunk of bread from Grandma Dracula's purse or maybe she's got a money box."

Fay said, "She tried to pump me last night, late. I don't think she bought that you're my half brother. I'm scared of her, Jay!"

He frowned, "Don't be scared, baby; be cool and smart. Soon that kitchen and this place ain't gonna be nothing but a memory. You remember to tell her what I told you?" he asked with a serious face.

She said, "No, I'm an idiot. So, I told her the truth, that I'm the runaway stepdaughter of one of the wealthiest assholes in Milwaukee, crazy enough to hook up with an Arkie from the coal pits and get busted for stealing five bucks worth of tamales."

They laughed.

She sighed, "My stepfather would pop off if I crawl back."

"Fay, I guarantee your horny pa ain't gonna get another shot at your poonie. And there ain't never gonna be no more coal pits for me, no more sweat for us, and no more missed meal cramps for us. We're gonna live cushy and hang tough and pretty in the tall sweet clover," he said with a grim face. "I'll figure a way, out there. Trust me!"

"I trust you, Jay, in clover or in poison ivy. I'll always be your girl and love you," she whispered as she sucked his bottom lip.

She turned and went to the door. Then she paused, blew a kiss, stepped into the hall, and shut the door.

He heard Big Ralph, the outside dorm keeper, bellowing profanely. He heard the raillery and shouts of the dozen-odd juvenile delinquents as they washed up for breakfast. He shuddered to remember himself out there with them about to start a long day in the fields beneath a blowtorch July sun. Worse than the coal pits, he told himself. Moments later, he heard the six kitchen and laundry girls in the attic dorm above preparing to start their day and the acid tongue of Phoebe, the old dorm mother.

A half hour later, Jay tensed, felt his heart jump cycle to hear the weird old foster mother stir and the usual strange sounds from her room on the first floor below his. He got out of bed and put his ear to the vent. Her demonic gabbling shivered his spine as always. Beneath it, he heard the dulcet warble of canaries. Then he retched from a horrible meld of piercing, hissing sounds and the terrified shrieks of canaries. "Cobra!" he said aloud.

"Homer! You share with Abigail, you heah?" he heard her say sharply. Then after several moments of silence, he heard her order, "Back to your straw now, gluttons!" Then she cooed, "That's my lovelies."

He heard the door shut, so he went to put an ear against his door to hear Grandma on the stairs. He got into bed. He shuttered his enormous blue eyes, limped his nude steel wire frame in fake sleep. Impregnated coal dust mascara rimming his eye sockets gave his gold-mopped face a debauched cast.

Moments later, he trembled uncontrollably at the sound of his room's doorknob twisting stealthily. Through blinds of silky lashes he saw the door open. Her jowly, corrupt face was thickly rouged and lipsticked. Her massive flab was silhouetted through a red silk wrapper as she stood in the doorway. Her widow's peak and frame of the robe reflected her ruined, long-nosed visage, which gave her a chilling satanic presence. Her wrists and arms were scarred by fang punctures.

She held a glass of orange juice in her hand. She concealed the whip, looped on her wrapper belt, at her back. Smoothly, she shut the door with a bump of her epic rump and padded toward the bed.

Jay heard Fay and the other girls chattering in the hallway on their way to the kitchen downstairs. He shut his eyes tightly, and his hands knotted fists beneath the sheet. He heard the torrid rasp of the old voluptuary's breathing as she moved through the gloom to the side of the bed to his back and placed the glass on the nightstand, the whip on the carpet beside the bed.

The bed springs jounced as she slid her musky heat against him. A bluebonnet blossom rhinestone pinned into the dyed flame of her mane tickled excruciatingly as she nuzzled his spine and buttocks.

He willed himself numb. He'd pleaded a bellyache two nights ago to send her away frustrated and evil, muttering threats to return him to the fields or to juvenile authorities if he couldn't be sweet to her after all she had done for him. Now, she was back to grope him again, he thought. He'd never be able to get the money for his escape with Fay out with the field slaves in the dorm. Or worse, in jail.

Oh shit! I wish this horny creep would gimme a break. Drop dead or something, he thought. He ground his knuckles into his eye sockets as he flipped and yawned spuriously.

"Good morning, gorgeous," she crooned in whiskey contralto. "Look at me."

He stared at the ceiling, terrified of her green hypnotic orbs. "Morning, Grandma," he mumbled. He started to reach across her for his cigarettes on a nightstand. Her gem-spangled hand pressed him back.

As she tapped a cigarette from the pack to light, she pouted her lupine lips. "Please, babykins, call me Brandy," she entreated as she flicked flame to the cigarette and laid it between his lips.

She took a jeweled hash pipe from her wrapped pocket, lit it, and pulled on it with slumberous eyes for a long moment. The smoke rode the air pungently as she exhaled. "Oh, Gawd, it's wonderful!" she exclaimed.

She took his cigarette, tapped ash off it into an ashtray, then pressed the pipe stem between his lips. He hesitated.

She crooned, "Hit it a drag, Angel Face. It will give you wings."

He drew deeply, coughed.

She said, "Draw easy, deep, babykins."

He closed his eyes and sucked on the pipe. She swooped and licked his washboard belly and jogged her tongue in his nipple. Then she lay gazing spellbound at his movie star profile as he sucked on the pipe and stared at the cigarette smoke rings she blew toward the ceiling.

His awesome comeliness sparkled her ancient crotch. This cute enticer is prettier than Billy Dove, the cruel bastard that I turned my first trick for, she thought. I've got to sculpt his head in plaster for a bronze! She pulled the wrapper off her head. Her scarlet fingernails knifed his pubic thicket. She noticed his organ activate a bit.

He passed the pipe. The hash swirled him into a downer. He remembered the pigsty jail and his yearlong week with the others in the field.

She licked his mouth. He was rigid as he struggled not to recoil. She turned away for an instant to put the pipe on the nightstand. Quickly, he wiped his mouth with the back of his hand. He remembered that the field slaves called her "Grandma Randy the Witch" behind her back.

He darted a glance at her mountainous lobster pink ruin, tree trunk legs scabrous with varicose veins. A combination of pity and revulsion panged him as he thought of the slew of nearly nude G-stringed images in her bedroom, on the walls, tables, and dresser depicting her reign, forty years before, as Bluebonnet Brandy Hoffstader, the sleek honky-tonk queen of Galveston stripper-prostitutes.

He giggled as he told himself a rhyme: "Grandma Brandy now ain't dandy. Just fat and randy."

She said, "Li'l darlin', it's like music to hear you laugh."

He panned her bulk with mocking eyes. He snickered, then he laughed uncontrollably. She stared at him malevolently, bit him hard on a nipple. He gasped, reflexively back-handed her face. Through the hash swoon, the face of his cruelly lustful grandmother, Binnie, flashed in his head like neon.

He trembled, with mouth agape, as he stared at her. "Bin . . . uh . . . Grandma, please! Don't! Please! I mean it!"

But she noticed an odd telltale passion in his eyes. She grinned like a shark as she rubbed her jaw and observed his organ quiver to half erection for an instant. Her eyes were radiant with excitement. She turned and palmed a diamond wristwatch with a gem-cut band of gold squares from her wrapper pocket on the carpet. With a smile, she turned toward him. With plump fingertips, she dangled and swept it before his eyes. The bauble shot like golden stars. His blue eyes followed the path of the glittery pendulum hypnotically.

She whispered, "It's yours, li'l darlin'."

He mumbled, "Mine, Gran . . . uh . . . Brandy?"

She sucked the end of his tip-tilted nose as she slipped it on his wrist.

"It's yours because you're so beautiful and I flat-out adore you," she whispered hoarsely.

He twisted his wrist, gazed entranced at the shimmering treasure. "This cost five hundred at least," he murmured.

She smiled. "A thousand, my pet, plus tax."

He pecked her forehead and exclaimed, "Thanks! It's the most beautiful watch there ever was!"

She sweetly whispered, "It's nothing! My mother left me tons of money. When we're regular sweeties, you'll be spiffy in nothing less than suits, everything tops! Kiddo, I mean rocks on your fingers big as your heartbreaking eyes, your pockets stuffed with 'C' notes, a white Caddie convertible, with all the extras."

She heaved a sigh, "I can't wait to see you with it all. Honey, dearie, everything is up to you." She threw an elephantine thigh across his belly.

"What I got to do?" he whispered.

She patted his cheek. "Be my sweetie true and make me feel good."

He said, "Feel good? Like how?"

She said, "In a moment, dearie, I'll tell you like how."

She took the glass of orange juice, heavily laced with a powerful hypnotic drug, off the nightstand. She smiled. "Drink your breakfast juice to the most beautiful watch there ever was," she said as she extended the glass.

The hash and the excitement of the watch had parched him. He took the glass, sipped, then drained it thirstily. She smiled and relit the hash pipe and passed it to him. The watch continued to magnetize his eyes as he leeched on the pipe. He fell back relaxed and dreamy eyed.

She uncoiled the whip from the wrapper belt and moved it to the bed behind her. She finger-stroked him from head to toe, watchful for the moment to lynch his fledging manhood on her gallows of sadism. She used her fingertips at her throat and above her cheekbones to pull taut the liver-spotted sag of skin to get an instant, pathetic, almond-eyed face-lift.

She said, "Look! I'm going to be pretty too, when I get the works from you, darlin'."

He darted a glance at the gargoyle and averted his eyes to the treasure on his wrist.

She moved cold eyes into his face. "Would you believe your so-called sister wasn't in my class for looks when I was a girl? Look at me!"

His heart drummed as he stared at her with glazed eyes. He slurred, "Sure, I believe. You're still cute, Gran . . . uh . . . Brandy, like a China doll. Now, like what do I gotta do to get the dough and Cad and stuff?"

She scowled as her hand derricked up a withered blob of purple-veined, forty-eight breast. She scooted up and rubbed its spoiled cherry nipple against his cheek. Her voice shook. "Like now, suck this goodie is how you start to be my sweetie."

He felt his belly roil, felt chained and paralyzed. He looked at her with piteous eyes and shook his head in slow motion. "I don't feel good, feel funny, feel like I ain't me," he murmured.

She reached behind her and gripped the whip then slid off the bed, stood, and growled. "I'm going to chastise you to make you sweet." She grunted for velocity and hacked the whip across his crotch.

He rolled away, howled piercingly with a breaking quaver like the child he was when he first felt the savage lash of a whip. The old woman's whip whistled a vicious lyric as she flogged him mercilessly.

Drug-shackled in a time warp, he jerked himself from a fetal ball and lay supine. He whimpered in a child's voice, "Please don't beat me no more, Binnie! I'll obey, I'm your slave!"

Her face leaked rivulets of dripping sweat, clownish with streaked rouge and mascara. He erected as the whip stung a rash of scarlet welts. At the moment of the spewing of his ejaculation, she lowered herself across the bed and kissed and bit his lips savagely as he yelped.

She stood with a ferocious face. "Get down here on your knees and lick my feet!" she commanded.

He blubbered incoherently as his dope-maimed body laboriously scuttled from the bed to the carpet on his knees before her. He dipped his head and feverishly kissed and licked her feet.

She slashed his buttocks with the whip. "Now, tongue pussy!" she commanded in a harsh voice.

He buried his face in her gray, scraggly sex-nest until rapture hooded her eyes. Her teeth gnashed as she yowled. Her obese knees quivered, and she collapsed, panting, onto the bed. He buried his face in a pillow and gnawed it as he cried.

She stared at him with tender eyes for a long moment, then she leaned and stroked his hair. He cringed away. She staggered as she got to her feet. Grunting, she half-lifted him onto the bed on his stomach. She took baby oil from her wrapper pocket and gently applied it to his wounds.

She rubbed her cheek against his hard belly and crooned, "You're so goddamn adorable, dearie. I'm gonna adopt you with papers, and flat-out marry you the second you're old enough. You're mine! Now, lie and rest long as you want; don't polish the car or anything. You only got to help me with my corset when I go out later today. That won't be until around noon."

She quivered with murderous eyes as she stared at a strand of Fay's platinum hair snared in his crotch bush. Her fingers curled into long, nailed claws to rake his face. Instead, she stood, slipped on her wrapper, and waddled from the room, her face hideous with anger.

He lay in a fire-bed of pain, with tearstained face, his thighs gluey with semen. He slugged the pillow and silently screamed he'd kill her. Through the dope haze, he relived the crunch of fate's trap with zoom-shot fidelity:

He saw himself grimy, belly growling with hunger several days off a freight train. He'd been lying on a pallet of rags in the twilighted basement of a condemned house near the Galveston waterfront used by a mob of homeless street urchins like himself between panhandling missions and thieving forays for food and garbage wine. He was rising from his odious bed, salivating at the thought of another grab-and-run score from the cart of one of the street food vendors when the basement entrance was suddenly shadowed.

A half-dozen tattered basement denizens shoved Fay into the basement at knifepoint. Her eyes were phosphorescent blue globes of terror in the purple murk. Her teeth chattered, lips batted mute protest as they pushed her to the basement floor on her back and ripped off her panties. The older husky leader stripped off his pants and dropped between her palsied thighs with a stiff dingus and his knife at her throat. The others undid their flys and lined up in the humping order of their ages and/or brawn.

Jay stared, paralyzed with shock, as the leader stroked brutally into his victim, whose piteous sobbing vibrated the basement. He was galvanized to take violent action when the rapist slugged Fay's face with his fist. He fumbled in his bed of rags for his weapon of fat steel pipe, gripped it, and lunged to the attack.

The line hollered warning as he smashed the pipe against the top of the leader's head. He rolled off limply and vacant-eyed. The others snarled and crowded in, muttering profane threats, with organs waggling, as he pulled Fay to her feet. He and Fay backed into a corner as the mob moved in.

He slashed the pipe through the air at their heads and screamed, "I'll break your fucking heads! Get back, motherfuckers! We're coming out!"

They retreated a few feet blocking the exit. He clutched Fay's hand as he moved toward them brandishing the pipe. His teeth bared like fangs in his feral face, contorted like a wolverine's protecting its cub. The mob scattered away before his doomsday countenance. He and Fay escaped down an alley to a jalopy cadaver in a slum street a dozen blocks away.

He saw anew the blistered shell that became his and Fay's love-nest home for the two weeks they roved, stole, and begged in the streets of Galveston's waterfront district. To protect her against further assault, they posed as sister and brother, and they were inseparable except for hygienic and biological moments in service station washrooms.

He remembered that last, half-starved, early evening in the crowded streets when they had sneaked up behind a tamale vendor as he gave change to a customer. They scooped handfuls of tamales off a steam grid on his cart into paper sacks and fled toward an alley mouth. They ran, pursued by the elderly Mexican vendor, smack into a police cruiser easing from the alley. They were arrested at gunpoint and taken to the juvenile lockup.

Jay remembered how many of his jailhouse acquaintances received indeterminate sentences for petty theft from the hanging judge presiding, even sentences up to twenty-one years.

Vividly he recalled how Grandma had come the day before his scheduled court appearance. He remembered how she had selected him and several other boys like heads of cattle from the juvenile tank, to save them from the state reformatory she'd told them. He had refused Grandma's generosity unless his half sister, Fay, was rescued as well. Politically clouted Grandma was cunning all right, he thought. She had rescued them for free labor on her ranch and in her fields as house servants and lackeys behind the twenty-foot barbed wire-topped fence of her foster home-stockade.

Now, easing into slumber, he told himself, "I'll be smooth, cool, and case our escape from Monsterville."

## III

Dream shrouded, Jay crept up behind Grandma, securing the bluebonnet blossoms in her hair at the top of the steep second-floor landing. He was panting and wild-eyed as he cat-footed close enough to see sproutings of white hair at the roots of the strawberry red mass. He raised the flat of his foot, drew his knee back to his chest, and sighted on the porcine small of her back. He heard his knee crack as he launched his foot like a missile into her back.

He clapped his palms over his ears to blot out her screaming as she bounced and tumbled down the stairs, making terrible pulpy sounds. He stared at her motionless, twisted bulk at the bottom of the stairs. Shards of blood-speckled bone thrust starkly from her askew neck as she gazed up at him accusingly for seeming eons.

Then she pulled herself to her feet and daintily pressed all, except one, of the shards back into place. She snatched that one free. Slowly, she popped her head and crooked neck straight with the heel of her hand. He stood transfixed as she ascended to him brandishing the shard like a dagger.

She said, "Naughty, naughty. Turn your palms up for punishment, li'l darlin'."

He watched her very gently spank his upturned palms with the bloody shard in the manner of a grade school teacher with a ruler.

He cried out again and again, "I didn't really want to kill you, Grandma!"

She smiled as she continued the spanking and recited softly like a poem, "You can't kill Brandy 'cause you're not that handy. You can't put me away. Never. I'll come back to punish you forever and ever."

He screamed, "I swear, Grandma, it was an accident! I stumbled against you!"

Her face became fearsome with rage as she inserted the shard into her neck. Then she seized and violently shook his shoulders. "Don't lie to Brandy! I can read your mind!" Her long nose touched his.

He thrashed on the shadowy precipice between sleep and reality.

"Wake up, dearie!"

Reality pummeled his eyes open. He rolled away in a lather of sweat, in terror to see Grandma shaking him with a half-hooked corset clinging to her clumps of fat, looming above him.

She smiled knowingly. "I heard you raving murder, dearie. You're stupid to waste yourself dreaming to kill me. You can't!" She leaned her mouth close to his ear. "Kiddo, Brandy is Satan's pet!" she whispered sibilantly as if she had emerged with him from the nightmare.

He slid to the carpet, eyes averted from the soul-deep probing of her green orbs chilling his entrails. After ten sweaty minutes, he pressed and hooked her into the heavy-ribbed corset. She rewarded him for the monumental accomplishment with a kiss on his nose.

He'd wondered about the scars. Now, he stared mesmerized by the fang wounds on her lower arms gleaming lividly in the sunlight.

She pinched his cheek and laughed. "I have adorable pets, li'l darlin', that, unfortunately, are flat-out ornery at times." She grinned ruefully as she stroked an arm. "But, I've long since become immune to their . . . uh . . . naughtiness. Bless their rapscallion hearts."

His voice trembled. "Pets!? Why do you want slimy sn—?"

She tapped his lips with an index finger. "Hush! My pets are not your affair, you heah, dearie?" she said sharply.

She retrieved a Polaroid camera off the nightstand and stared at him thoughtfully for a long moment. "Li'l darlin', get into your spiffy pastel blue suit."

He went to the closet and got it from the rack holding a half-dozen other noisy western suits she'd bought.

He said, "I need a shower."

She waved her arm imperiously. "Oh, forget that. I'm pressed for time. Now, put it on and let's get some shots."

He put on the suit with grey boots, then brushed his long golden locks at the dresser mirror. He tied a grey silk scarf around his neck. Her hand jiggled his crotch to free his organ from between his thighs for imprint beneath the fabric of his tight pants.

"I'm flat-out going to have myself a ball flashing his gorgeous pictures on that bitch Saint Tiffany," she told herself with perverse glee.

She arranged his limbs and head for a series of sexy macho poses. For twenty minutes she stooped and lumbered about him until she had a stack of shots from many angles.

"In our private oven you'll find pork chops and gravy, with biscuits I fixed for you," she said as she sat on the side of the bed shuffling and examining the pictures.

He went across the hall and ran through the shower. She was standing in the bathroom doorway when he emerged, beaded and glistening. She watched him wince as he gingerly toweled himself dry. She sighed, kissed the welts on his back, and turned away down the hallway for the stairs.

He got on the throne and gazed at his watch. It twinkled noon. He cocked his head and admired the bauble with bright eyes and twisted his wrist to hype up the sparkle of the dial stones.

As he dressed in his gold-ivory, white deep-pile carpeted room, his empty belly growled, but he decided to stay upstairs until she left. He heard the roar of the field truck and the cry of its brakes. He went to the window overlooking the dorm. He felt bandboxical, showered, cologned, and dap in a fresh beige suit. Grizzled, carrot-topped Big Ralph heaved himself from the truck and unlocked the tailgate.

Jay watched the sun-scorched rabble of teenagers leap from the truck, whooping joy for the Saturday half-day respite from the stoop agony chopping of the cotton plants free of weeds. Pungent zephyrs of sweat and manure stung his nostrils through the open window. Their grit-measled faces and the mute explosions of dust grenades from their coveralls, as they stampeded for the bathhouse behind the dorm, panged him with pity. He drew a sigh and wished them all house pets like himself. Without Grandma, he amended.

He heard a distinctive snort of bellicosity above the "moo" bedlam of market steers milling in the cattle pens beyond the dorm. He glimpsed in the corral the buck-stomp violence of Hitler, the mad bronc Big Ralph was prepping to break. He gazed at the free world crawl of insect cars on the highway, the sun-glinted barbed wire fence beyond the ocean of peek-a-boo cotton blossoms soon to explode from emerald buds.

The sound of Grandma's Lincoln gunning at the front of the mansion caused him to tense. He crossed the hall to the bathroom window. She was moving the pearl machine past profusions of blue-bonnet blossoms down the driveway toward the steel gate in the barbed wire fence, a hundred-odd yards distant. He saw the gate, activated by an electronic control inside the car, slide open on its tracks, then bang-lock behind her as she tooled the new car onto the roadway. He returned to his room to protect himself against snake-bite. He put on gloves and picked up a softball bat.

He hastened down the circuitous hallway to the stairway and descended quietly to the ground-floor hallway. He started down the hallway back toward Grandma's bedroom beneath his at the rear of the house. He paused to peep at the blue-jeaned crew of girls, on cigarette break, in the spacious kitchen. They were dewy faced from vapors of odorous steam spewing from gigantic pots of lunch stew aboil on the range. He exchanged smiles with Fay.

As elderly Phoebe turned from checking loaves of bread in the oven, he moved away to Grandma's spring-locked bedroom door. Careful not to scratch the doorjamb, he shimmied the latch back with his pocketknife. He thought of Grandma's fang wounds. His knees shook as he eased the door open and stood at the threshold to accustom his eyes to the heavily draped murk.

A trio of Grandma's sculpted plaster images of fiends and murderers lurked in a cluster on a platform behind the black velvet headboard of an emperor-sized bed. He stepped into the room and locked the door. Mister Hyde, Landru, and Count Dracula, neatly attired in period costumes, glowed hideously in a soft ray of hidden blue light.

Jay stared at the apparitions as he moved across the room to the windows and opened the black velvet drapes halfway. He stood in the blast of sunlight, exhaled tension. He swept his eyes about the clutter of antique furniture, multisized statuary, cardboard boxes bulged with old clothes, yellowed magazines and newspapers. Half-nude pictures of young Brandy infested the room.

He gingerly probed the bat beneath the bed to flush out Grandma's pets. He went to the locked closet. He saw straw fragments on the carpet. He rattled the doorknob and heard a rustling sound when he put his ear against the door.

He started his escape-cash search in the crammed drawers of a massive mahogany dresser. He burrowed fruitlessly through musty piles of mildewed finery for fifteen minutes before he found a dozen keys on a ring. He sat on a prickly horsehair chair twirling the key ring as he caught his breath.

Jay looked about the room for possible stashes and spied the legs of a squat piece of furniture shrouded by an indigo opera cape, mottled with dust. He went and uncovered a filigreed cabinet. He tried several keys in its lock before the doors swung open. The interior, stacked tight with books, legal papers, and photo albums, belched a foul gust of aged air.

He stared at, then reached toward, a thin book on the Science of Embalming. Instead, he pulled out a heavy, tattered book, riffled through half the pages for a greenback cache before he halted and stared at a drawing of a disemboweled woman on a stone altar surrounded by a ghoulish mob with maniacal faces. He looked at the book's cover: Immortality Through the Power of Satanism. He completed his search of the book.

He replaced it and opened a gold-leafed photo album. A sheaf of yellowed newspaper clippings magnetized his attention. He read several.

The first was an account and shot of how beautiful rebel stripper Brandy Hoffstader had excoriated, cursed, and spat in the socialite face of Otto, her father, on a Galveston cabaret stage when he had interrupted her performance with righteous indignation. The audience was seen applauding riotously.

Another clipping: The headlined account of the barbiturate suicide of Constance Hoffstader, civic leader and social queen. Her suicide note condemned her husband, Otto, as her murderer via his long-term bestial treatment of her and Brandy and his numerous illicit affairs with other women.

Jay unfolded a full page of lurid story, with pictures, on Tiffany Hoffstader, Brandy's twin sister. She, the possessor of impeccable reputation and social status, had descended into the pit of madness when jilted by her socialite inamorata. She waited, in her bridal gown, in the crowded church for the groom who had married someone else hours before. Family members reported that she had disappeared.

Jay searched the cabinet and found no cash. He restored the

contents and locked the cabinet. Then he searched every inch of the room, except the closet lair of Grandma's pets. He drew the drapes. "My only hope for escape dough is her purse," he told himself. He left the room and pulled the door shut and locked.

As he went down the hall, he nearly tinkled on himself when Fay said, "Boo!" as she grabbed his arm and pulled him into the deserted kitchen.

He frowned. "Stop the pranks, Fay! Huh?"

She tiptoed and kissed the corner of his glum mouth. "You score?" she whispered.

"Not a red cent in that funk box. I'll take a shot at her purse first chance," he said wearily.

"Everyone is out in the mess hall. Let's slip upstairs and make love," she said breathlessly.

He shook his head. "No good, not cool with the monster probably on the turn. Besides, I'm hungry," he said as he went to the small private gas stove in a corner.

He took his plate of gravied pork chops, rice, and biscuits from the oven. She sat with him in the breakfast nook and watched him wolf the plate clean.

She said, "I gotta pin you down, sweetmeat. When we gonna do it?"

He grinned. "Tonight, late," he said as he rose and walked toward the doorway.

She followed, tugged at his sleeve. "When, late?"

He shrugged. "Midnight. Bang my ceiling to get the all-clear. Look, Ice Cream Cone, I feel bad vibes about the old creep. I think she knows you're not my sister. So let's be careful. You know, like let's don't be Siamese twins in the yard like we've been, OK?" he asked with a solemn face.

Her eyes twinkled mischief. "Okay. I'll give Marcus some action for our cover. Now, kiss me."

He took her into his arms and bit her lip for the Marcus crack.

Their tongues combated furiously for a long moment before he split for the corral.

## IV

Grandma, coruscating in her puce and peace tent of a silk dress, sat regally, triple-chinned, head high on a barstool in a Galveston cesspool. Bittersweet nostalgia panged Grandma as she remembered her reign as queen of the bump and grinders. She darted a glance behind her at the darkened stage of the former strip palace and Mecca for the cult of the artful tease.

She turned back and beamed a beatific smile down the bar at her claque of time-hacked subjects wallowing in the time warp of the good old days of fresh faces and wild, impossible dreams of breaking the gaffed casino of life. The good old days of wizard torsos when Bluebonnet Brandy was the supreme hard-on enticer with the mostest.

A bedraggled loser toasted, "Here's to Brandy, the sexiest fluff that ever peeled off and humped a runway."

The motley mob hoisted their shot glasses and flung the fifth round she'd sprung for down their cast-iron gullets.

She went to the juke box and dropped in quarters pursued by a derelict roue in quest of a sugar mama. He managed to lick her ear and whisper his raging passion to eat her twat before a rabid bouncer galloped him through the door by the seat of his well-ventilated pants.

She jiggled her lumpy hips to upbeat music in the manner of an erotic hippo as she gazed ecstatically at her reflected face in the mirrored interior of the box. In the sorcerous flattery of the rainbow glow of neon, abetted by time warp, she saw herself as the enchantress of old. My Gawd, old gal, you're still beautiful, she told herself. I guess my new love is why.

She turned away to go back to her stool when the scintillating vision of her teenage rival, Fay, enveloped her mind in depression and rage. I won't lose him to that chippie. I'll bury her! she vowed venomously.

She felt embarrassing tears on the brink, so she dug in her purse for tab money. Then she went to the bar and tossed a pair of hundred dollar bills before the bartender. She managed to smile as she moved through a saccharine gauntlet of kisses, best wishes, and embraces on her way to her car at the curb.

She unlocked it and got in, then sat and stared at the bouquet of bluebonnets she'd cut to place on her mother's grave: The thirtieth anniversary of her suicide. She bombed the car away in a storm of tears and darted a glance at her face in the rearview mirror. The time-warped magic was gone, and she was ugly Grandma again with bloodshot eyes. She bellowed self-pity and grief as she stomped the purring horses to a hundred-miles-per-hour pace.

A state trooper's cruiser siren growled behind her. She slowed the Lincoln to a legal forty. The trooper flashed his dome lights. She set her jaw and didn't pull over. The trooper drew abreast, peered sternly at her for an instant, then grinned apologetically through his open window. She ran her window down.

"Howdy-do, Grandma. Didn't recognize you in your new machine. Be careful! See ya, ma'am."

She nodded tipsily as he pulled away, then drove at ninety several miles to a wooded cemetery. A silver-thatched curmudgeon left a kiosk to swing open a wide metal gate. Grandma drove through a grove of chinaberry and pecan trees to an imposing black marble mausoleum with Constance Hoffstader, date of birth, and death chiseled in giant Gothic letters into its entry arch. She parked and entered its utter silence and placed the bouquet of bluebonnets on the silver casket.

Tears welled as she stared at the gleaming box and shook her head. "Oh, Mama! I'm so lonely, so sorry I didn't realize how much you meant to me. Forgive me, darlin'! Your baby loves you, Mommy!"

She broke down in wild weeping and stumbled out to the roadway. Her tear-wet face congealed to vindictive hardness as she walked fifty yards up the road to stop before a tall headstone gutted with weeds: Otto Hoffstader and date of birth and death were chiseled into the gray granite. The wind sighed mournfully through the overhanging branches of a chinaberry tree. Her face was a twisted, bitterly hateful mask as she stared at the sunken sod of the grave.

She sank to her knees atop it, lowered her face, and whispered ferociously, "I hated you living. I hate you dead and stinking. You rotten bastard! You heah!?"

She struggled to her feet, walked away a dozen paces, turned back, and screamed piercingly, "I hate you! I hate you!"

Birds in the chinaberry tree panicked and flapped away. She went to the car and drove to the public road. Ten minutes later, she drove into the parking area of a high-walled private sanitarium where she parked and made up her face.

She went into the red stone building past harried white-garbed attendants in a moil of middle-aged and elderly patients walking and wheel-chairing themselves through the sterile corridors and walked toward the administrative office. A receptionist showed her into the superintendent's stained-cedar paneled office.

A naked-pated ox of a man with a cherub's face rose from behind his cluttered desk. He beamed an IOU-fifty-grand smile. "How have you been, Brandy?" he chortled as he nervously hunched his shoulders inside his raucous Glen plaid suit and extended a brawny paw.

She placed her hand in his for an instant. "Not bad for an old bitch, Wesley," she said as she sat in a large chair before the desk.

"You look lulu lovely, my dear," he said as he lowered himself into his high-backed leather chair and eased a racing form into a drawer.

"Snow the chippies, old buddy," she said harshly.

She took a cigarette from her platinum case. Before she could flick flame to it, he leaned and lit it with a desk lighter. She blew a gust of smoke into his face as he reclined.

From her purse, she removed a letter and waved it. "Wesley, I'm so pissed with you I could bust your bald, irresponsible noggin wide open," she said in a deadly whisper as she flung the letter into his lap. "Read it!" she ordered as he picked it up and stared at it slack-jawed.

His face was creased with dismay when he finished reading it and passed it back to her.

"It was addressed to the governor. This is dynamite! She revealed her true identity and pleaded for a sanity hearing. How on earth did you intercept it?" he choked out.

"That's my business. I helped that trick become governor. I can take a shit on the state house carpet if I want. But that isn't the point." She leaned forward and gritted her teeth. "Your carelessness permitted my sister to smuggle out that letter. To the world she's dead. Wesley, she's got to stay that way. Understand? I want your staff, from dishwashers to physicians, interrogated and shaken up until they find the nosy sonuvabitch that mailed that letter for her!" She stood.

He stood and said, "I'll discover and fire whoever it is. I promise."

She moved to the door. "You've got a week." She studied his face. "You're not sucker enough to feel sorry for her are you, Wesley?"

He waved his palms through the air. "Not a twit of that. Like Justice, I've been blind for your cause, my dear, for twenty years," he said with a subtle edge of sarcasm, as he thought, I'll release her the day you kick the bucket, you fiend. "My loyalty has always been with you, dear heart," he crooned.

She opened the door. "Don't pancake on me, Wesley. As of last week I acquired sixty percent of Merchant Bank stock and the board chair. Your mortgage payments are a year delinquent, plus you owe me fifty grand. I'll foreclose on this white elephant booby hatch and convert it into a brothel and put you in charge of douche bags and washing dirty towels to work out my fifty grand," she said as she shut the door and went past the receptionist into the corridor.

She moved leisurely to Tiffany's second-floor private room savoring the turning of fate's cards that afforded her such sweet revenge. She fondled and knifed herself with memories of Tiffany luxuriating in the sun of her father's favor and affection while she festered and hated in exile. She remembered her father's ceaseless reprimands, rejection, and cruelty.

"Why can't you be a refined little lady like Tiffany instead of a stupid destructive brat?" he'd said that early morning after she'd awakened him and shown him her seven-year-old genius and love.

She had taken his hand and led him, in his yellow silk pajamas (she remembered), to his custom-made lizard golfing bag and clubs laid out neatly on the garden grass to dry in the embryo sun. He'd gasped and purpled as he stared at miniature likenesses of herself she'd painted on the bag and club shafts in bright vermillion with neat aqua Palmer method inscriptions: BRANDY LOVES DADDY. He'd seized her and beaten her bottom raw with a club shaft, then locked her into a black pit garage until noon.

When her chronically ailing mother returned the next day from the hospital, Brandy tearfully reported the beating and imprisonment. She remembered her mother was ambulanced back to the hospital that same day after a furiously profane shouting bout with her father.

In her early teens her father criticized her makeup, dates, and personality. "You're going to be a low-life gutter tramp! Use Tiffany as a role model. Save yourself!" he'd screamed until she was convinced, at eighteen, that he was indeed a prophet after his attacks drove her from home to street poisoning.

Her suicidal mother had grown too disturbed to protect her. But, at least she'd had the exquisite satisfaction of spitting on his corpse twelve years later in the mortuary viewing room one midnight.

Now, she eased open the room door of her father's paragon. Saint Tiffany, the magnificent and pure, she thought as she stepped into the sunny room. She smiled and looked into the green eyes of her snow-capped, gowned genetic mint replica lying in bed holding a book. The agony and stress of confinement had accomplished the same ruin and obesity that wanton freedom had inflicted on Grandma.

"Tiff, you look great!" Grandma exclaimed.

"Thank you, Brandy. It's good to see you," she said with a cultivated soft voice.

They pecked cheeks and embraced. Grandma sat on the side of the bed. Tiffany slid the book beneath the covers.

Grandma said, "Do you mind, kiddo?" as she scooped Henry Miller's Tropic of Cancer from concealment. Her eyes widened in ersatz shock. "My Gawd, dearie! Why, I just flat-out can't imagine a lady like you reading this notorious and immoral novel."

Tiffany blushed and averted her eyes. "A neighbor . . . a friend gave it to me . . . insisted that I read it," she stammered.

Grandma spanked Tiffany's hip. "A man friend, kiddo?"

Tiffany nodded.

Grandma leered. "He's hauling your hot ashes, maybe?"

Tiffany shook her head vigorously. "He's married. Just my friend. How is your love life out there in the big bright world?"

Grandma said, "I'm glad you asked," as she took the Polaroid shots of Jay from her purse and flung them onto Tiffany's abdomen.

Tiffany picked them up and looked at the first one. She threw her hand over her heart and gasped, "This young man looks incredibly like Cecil!"

Grandma said, "Only that li'l humper's ass is pretty enough to make Cecil a Sunday face. That's my new sweetie!"

Tiffany's hands shook as she examined the pictures. "He's just a child," she murmured. "There can't be a future with him. Can there be?"

Grandma leaned and snatched the pictures. One of them slipped down in the covers at Tiffany's hip. Grandma took the cue to stab in the knife.

"Future?" she laughed. "He's aching to get married when he's older. Why that li'l jock is got the hots for me so bad I've got to dose his food with saltpeter." She paused to twist the knife. "He may look like Cecil, kiddo, but I'll give you ten to five he won't leave his sweet patootie crying at the church."

Tiffany stricken eyes gazed about the monotonous off-white walls and ceiling. Her lips trembled as she burst into tears.

"Stop the waterworks, dearie pie," Grandma said sweetly as she moved to embrace Tiffany.

Tiffany scuttled away. "Please! Don't touch me! You hate me!"

Grandma stood and laughed. "Hate you, dearie? Why say a hurting thing like that? You're never going to get out of here feeling and thinking crazy like that."

Tiffany scooted up to a sitting position, tear-flooded eyes ablaze. "We know I'm not crazy, don't we? You don't want me out of here, but you're in for a surprise soon."

Grandma screwed her face into an anguished mask. She wiped her eyes with a handkerchief from her sleeve and sniffled, "You're so cruel and ungrateful after all I've done to get your release." She blubbered as she turned and left the room. A flower vase shattered against the door as she shut it.

She went down the corridor to the elevator; she smiled to see several attendants rush, with a straitjacket, toward the pandemonium of shrieking and crashing of window glass sounds from Tiffany's room.

Twilight's lavender blindfold had covered the sun's stark eye when Grandma parked in downtown Galveston. She walked through a crowd of Saturday shoppers and early on-the-towners into a posh jewelry store.

A clerk descended on her at the threshold. She selected a fiery cluster of diamonds on a gypsy mounting packaged in a gold satin box and paid with a fifteen hundred dollar personal check. Then she went to a drugstore several shops down the street to see a pharmacist friend where she purchased a bottle of chloroform.

As she pulled the Lincoln away for home in total euphoria she merrily hummed an old stripper's show tune.

## V

In the deepening twilight, Jay lay groaning on his belly naked.

Fay gently massaged liniment into his bruised body. "Damn!

Your back and ass, besides the bruises, look like you've been whipped. The welts!"

He growled, "You saw how I tumbled and slid when that maniac bronc threw me. Those are scratches, not whip welts. Now, get the hell out of here before the witch brooms home."

Fay kissed his neck and stood. "Well, I guess the bronc kicked my loving date in the head for tonight," she sighed as she went to the door.

He winced as he leapt spastically out of the bed to prove his indestructible macho. He said stoutly as he embraced her waist, "By midnight, I'll be back in the almost pink. So, knock the ceiling at midnight, okay?"

She kissed him. "Okay. But even if you're not up to par, I can always ride the peg."

They laughed and sucked tongues. Then Fay went down the hall-way toward the attic dorm stairs. Jay shut the door and hobbled to the window. He lit a cigarette and watched Hitler, the bronc, rearing and kicking in the corral. "I'll break your black ass down like a ten buck shotgun soon as I heal," he told himself.

He had limped back to bed when Grandma opened his door. She stood in the doorway sniffing. Then she walked in and sat on the side of the bed.

"I hate liniment! You hurt?" she said, wiggling her nose.

"Yeah, bad as I can with no broken bones," he moaned to block any of her amorous notions.

"Who was sweet enough to rub you down, dearie?" she asked as she lit a cigarette.

"Me, who else?" he answered too hastily and desperately.

"Your sister, kiddo. That's who," she said with slitted eyes that yo-yoed his Adam's apple.

"Naw, she's under the weather herself, I think."

Grandma kissed his cheek and stood. She yawned. "I'm bushed and sleepy myself. You've got a peach of a gift, li'l darlin', I bought you. Maybe it tops the watch."

He said, "Nothing except a Caddie convertible could top the watch. What you got for me, Brandy?"

She said, "I'll bring it with me tomorrow when I get my sugar refill." Then she opened the door, stepped out into the hallway, and closed the door. Minutes later, he heard a rap on the door. Shit! Main Street pad! he thought.

"Come in," he said.

Big Ralph, decked out in a grey houndstooth suit and snowy ten-gallon hat, peacocked into the room with his moon face hedgerowed with concern.

"How ya doin', Baby Slim?" he said as he walked to the side of the bed.

Jay faked a smile. "Shoot, I was just thinking about saddling up black-ass Hitler for another go-round before it got real dark."

They laughed.

"You got the heart and the touch to be a sonuvabitching performer one day. Your steer wrestling and roping is the best I've seen a novice do. You wanta take a slice of advice from this old-timer?" Big Ralph said seriously.

"Sure, Big Un, you're my professor."

The giant said, "Broncs got radar and murder stuffed between their ears. Hitler got wise you was leery and tight in the saddle. You gotta stay tough but loose. You gotta flow and glow positive through the earthquakin'. Got it?"

Jay nodded.

Big Ralph gave him a feathery fist in the shoulder. "I'm goin' to town to destroy some whiskey. Want anything?"

Jay said, "Thanks, Big Un, but I got everything to keep me from going nuts for now."

They laughed. Big Ralph left the room.

A half hour before midnight, restless Fay lay bright eyed in the darkened quiet of the dorm. She watched summer breezes lash a chinaberry tree outside an open, screened window near her bed. Its branches cavorted spectral shadows on the moon-tinted walls.

Her chum, Millie from Dallas, in the bed beside hers, writhed. She pleaded piteously in her sleep. "Ah, mister! Please don't shoot! Let me go!" as she relived a kidnapping by a pervert-killer interrupted by police cars before he could dismember her as he had several other girls.

Fay shivered, felt a familiar spasm behind her belly button. The feeling shifted her mind to her middle-aged novelist stepfather and the fearful awful night several weeks after the childbirth deaths of her mother and premature sister. She remembered she'd been asleep around midnight in her bedroom in the palatial home of her stepfather in the Whitefish Bay section of Milwaukee. Her mother had married him two years before.

The stepfather, Frank, slid his naked body into bed with her, fondled her half awake. For several seconds she thought she was having a nightmare as she watched and felt him sucking her breast. He reeked of alcohol.

She screamed, "Goddammit, Frank, you gone nuts!" as she punched his head away and tried to escape from the bed.

He seized her and squeezed her close, showered her face with spittled drunken kisses as he passionately sobbed, "Your beauty has destroyed my will to live if I can't be your lover. I've failed my sacred vow to do without you, Angel Witch. Torturer Goddess, saboteur of my sleep and sanity, have mercy! You must understand! With Felicia gone from us, way out there beyond the heavens, we're like infant sparrows together, deserted in the snow. I'm bewitched! No price is too high to pay to have you. Disgrace? A pittance! Prison? A bagatelle!"

She raked his face, arms, and back bloody with her fingernails. Anesthetized by desire, he forced her thighs open, hunched his muscular two hundred and fifty pounds, and entered her. He punched her jaw. She dropped into a dark abyss. She revived and feebly continued to maim him with slashing fingernails and gouging teeth as he pumped away to climax.

He cursed and rolled off the bed to his feet. He went down the hall to the bathroom. She followed to peek through the keyhole. He was treating his wounds with iodine. Fay went back to her room, slipped into jeans, and snatched up her piggy bank before she fled the house.

She took the Greyhound to Galveston to look up her mother's cousin. She discovered that the cousin had moved to Alaska. Fay remembered with a shudder her penniless frightful week before Jay rescued her from gang-rape in the basement of the condemned house in Galveston.

Now, she tingled as she noticed one minute to midnight on the wall clock. She glanced at Phoebe, the dorm mother, fast asleep across the way. She eased out of bed, picked up a shoe, and went several feet to the furnace vent in the wall. She gently tapped the shoe heel against the floor. Shortly, she heard Jay tap his ceiling. Then his familiar kissy oral sex sound issued and spasmed her crotch.

"I'm going to come!" she stage-whispered down the vent.

Within the minute, she entered his room and slipped out of her gown. They moved the dresser against the door.

Grandma, in red wrapper, stepped with a feral face from the shadows at the bend of the hallway. She moved soundlessly down the hallway carpet past the tryst room in stocking feet to a guest room near the foot of the darkened attic dorm stairway.

She put the bottle of chloroform and a rag on the carpet near the door. Then she got a chair and sat down. Her face was suffused with rage in the flare of her lighter as she shakily lit a cigarette and peered at Jay's door through the cracked guest room door.

The young lovers settled for a near wipeout sixty-nine before a brief ride on Jay's peg. Panting, they lay smoking a cigarette between them. In the cathedral quiet, her child's face was poignantly innocent in a soft blue spot of moonlight.

"Candy Dong, know what kinda home I wish for when we get rich?"

He said, "Gimme a rundown, Ice Cream Cone."

She closed her eyes. "A pink house, definitely a shocking pink house on a hill. I mean a high one. A flower garden, a pink swimming pool shaped like your dong. A zillion kids your spitting image and servants by the battalions."

They laughed, clung together, kissed as if they had no tomorrows together before she slipped on her gown. They moved the dresser. She kissed him once more and left the room.

Goddamn, that broad has got me hooked, he thought, as he flung himself into bed and inhaled the odor of their love stew.

With pink ribbon in hair gleaming like a cache of Inca platinum, she skipped down the hall humming like the ecstatic child she was. She reached the dorm stairway and took a step when Grandma lunged from the guest room and seized her throat from behind. Fay made choking sounds as her blue eyes bulged out in pain and terror.

Grandma dragged her by the throat, kicking and squirming, into the guest room and dropped her three hundred pounds onto her frail prey to anchor her to the carpet, with a heavy knee on her throat to strangle outcry. She quickly saturated the rag with chloroform and pressed it against Fay's face until she went limp.

Grandma grabbed a foot and peeped down the hallway before she stepped out. Fay's dislodged pink hair ribbon lay on the door threshold. She dragged her victim down the hall past Jay's room. Fay's body against the carpet made only a whispery rustle like a snake's belly snagging on autumn leaves. Fay's head bounced quietly on the carpeted stairway to the ground floor, but sickeningly on the pine steps leading to the basement furnace room.

A sweet tooth had sent Jay to the private oven for Grandma's peach cobbler an eyelash second after Grandma had reached back to shut the basement door behind her. He was spooning cobbler into a dish when he heard the bumping sounds of Fay's head. He put the dish down and walked several feet down the hall to the basement door. He put his ear against it and heard sounds.

He stooped and peered through a hairline crack in the doorjamb. He saw only Grandma's back near the grinding machine and the usual clutter of dulled field hoes and rakes waiting to be sharpened. He sniffed at vapors of what he thought was chloroform. "Could Grandma be into an el cheapo high like that?" he asked himself.

He shrugged and went back to the cobbler. Sharpening of tools was his job. But what the hell, he thought. I'm her fucking house pet, so let the horny dingbat do my gig. He sat down and devoured three portions of cobbler and a quart of milk.

He stepped out of the kitchen and walked toward the stairway for the second floor. He retraced and put an eye to the hairline crack. He couldn't see her now. He put his ear to the door. No sounds.

He opened the door carefully and went down into the basement. She's not here, he thought, but where is she? I had to see her pass the kitchen unless Satan's pet has gone invisible.

He went to her open bedroom door. He went to his bedroom, stared into it. He opened the bathroom door. He walked to the guest room, flipped the light switch near the door. Empty. The stench of chloroform wrinkled his nose. He spotted the pink ribbon, stooped, and picked it up. "I'll kill her if she's hurt Fay," he told himself, as his chest inflated with tension.

He went to his bedroom and rapped the softball bat against his ceiling several times. No response. He decided to scout the dorm. But nausea churned his stomach, made him weak. Ill, his legs trembled as he went to sit on the side of the bed.

In a sub-cellar beneath the furnace room lit by a naked red bulb, Grandma had set up the embalming process on Fay. She was lying nude and ghastly white on a long table. A whirring machine sucked her bloodless through a tube inserted into an artery at the base of her crotch. A row of cheap caskets lay covered by a canvas cloth in a corner of the cave-like room.

Grandma leaned and pressed Fay's eyelids up with her fingertips. The eyes were blank, dead orbs. She grinned as she went to a short flight of stone stairs, ascended, and pressed a button on the sheet steel hatch on the sub-basement's ceiling.

A two-horsepower electric motor swung away hatch and ponderous grinding machine welded to it above. Grandma went through the aperture to the furnace room. She left the hole agape to go through the swinging doors of the basement john.

In the attic dorm, Jay stared down at Fay's empty bed. He crept through the silent dorm of sleeping girls and down the stairway. He went to his room and snatched up the baseball bat. Then he put on high boots and long-fringed cowboy gloves to his mid-arm. He went to the basement door, peeped, and listened before he tiptoed down the stairs. He saw the grinding machine out of position immediately. He went to the hole and stared down into it for a long moment.

Grandma watched him through the latticed doors of the toilet. Her eyes leaked tears as she watched her beloved pet disappear into the sub-chamber to seal his doom. She scrambled up the basement stairs to her bedroom. She unlocked the closet door.

Cobras, Homer and Abigail, slithered to her with affectionate low-key hisses. Grandma scooped them into her arms and started back to the basement.

Jay screamed grief as he crushed Fay's corpse against him at the table. "Please, Fay, baby! Come back! I can't live without you!"

He released her tenderly back on the table. His face was draconic as he went to a high stack of paper cartons and slugged them away with the bat hoping Grandma was crouched behind them. He ripped off the canvas covering the row of caskets. He recoiled at the sight of the embalmed corpses of five young boys lying nude as if asleep in the satin-lined boxes.

He spun at the sound of weeping to see Grandma standing at the stone steps with the cobras slung across her shoulders like a stole. A pitchfork gleamed wickedly in her hand. He stared mesmerized, speechless.

Grandma shook her head sadly as tears rolled down her cheeks.

"Why, oh, why did you have to go poking your doll nose into Brandy's business? I flat-out adore you, li'l darlin'. I bought you a diamond ring, a cluster of stones bigger than your heartbreaking eyes. Next month I was gonna order a white Caddie convertible with all the extras . . . was gonna let Big Ralph make you a rodeo star with the spiffiest gear and duds on the circuit. It's gonna break my loving heart to fix you for keeping forever."

She smooched the cobras and set them on the cement. "Sic him, lovelies!" she commanded.

Jay gripped the bat and crouched in a combat stance, tear-flooded eyes brilliant in the red murk.

The grey, black-marked assassins emitted a chilling high-octave-penetrating hissing sound as they elevated the fronts of their sinuous bodies. The movable flab of their neck skins puffed out hideously. Their eyes flamed like bronze-hued coals of fire. Two front glistening fangs and three smaller upper fangs behind gleamed in the hellish heads as they moved across the cement to strike.

Jay took a mighty bat shot at their awful heads moving toward him in tandem, but missed. They cunningly separated to attack his flanks. Jay backed into a cul-de-sac of stacked cattle feed grain bags. He stumbled on a canister of rat bait to fall flat on his back. The cobras halted for a long moment.

Grandma lumbered up behind her motionless hit pets brandishing her pitchfork as she squawked, "Sic him, lovelies!"

They lunged in to fang droplets of venom down his boots before he was able to scramble to the top of a grain bag stack. Homer and Abigail fixed phosphorescent bronze orbs on him as they reared their hooded heads toward him. Jay kicked off several of the bags that pinned the cobras' lower bodies against the cement floor.

Grandma cursed and popped sweat as she struggled to get her monumental flab through the narrow aperture of the cul-de-sac of tightly stacked bags of feed.

Jay leapt down and quickly jellied the heads of the trapped cobras with his bat. Grandma bellowed grief as she barred Jay's escape from the cul-de-sac with savage jabs of the pitchfork.

He moved toward her, swinging the bat violently and screaming, "Please don't make me kill you, Grandma! I'm gonna let the cops punish you. Get out of my way, Grandma!"

She sneered and squeezed her bulk through the narrow lane of feed bags. She jabbed the pitchfork at Jay's throat. He ducked a split second in time. There was a terrible crunch sound when he slammed the bat against the side of Grandma's head. Her shattered skull gouted blood. She wobbled like a gigantic top before she collapsed dead on the cement floor.

Jay shook uncontrollably as he stared down at the slain voluptuary. The bat slipped from his palsied hand. The thud of it against the cement startled him. Panic seized him, galvanized him to leap over the corpse and streak from the mansion.

Sobbing, he ascended a brambled rise to railroad tracks. He lay in adjacent underbrush for seeming ages until the engine headlamps to a freight train, bound for Houston, labored up the incline toward him. He galloped from cover and swung aboard an empty boxcar where he lay panting and staring down at Grandma's mansion of horrors vividly eerie in the glow of frosty blue starlight.

He wept wildly for his dead sweetie, Fay, for the embalmed corpses of the boys. The star glow ignited a razzle of icy fire on the diamond dial of the wristwatch Grandma had given him. He gazed at the gaudy bauble and wept anew for Grandma until his entrails dry-locked. For after all, she had, he realized, gifted him with the spiffiest wristwatch there ever was.

# THE RECKONING

Ambushed by grief, San Francisco barmaid Lela Leseur left her post to weep behind the door of a washroom cubicle for several minutes. Composed, she walked to the mirror to renovate her makeup and to drop Murine into her reddened grey eyes. She returned to serve the midnight mob with a congealed, pained smile on her elfish Creole face.

The nicotine and perfume-choked air vibrated with profane jive and shuck of street people scoring the red-lit haze with a light show of jewelry and psychedelic clothes. Lela's pinch bottle curves inflated black satin leotards. She mesmerized a gallery of covetous eyes as she moved sensuously behind the long bar with two male bartenders.

At closing time, the five-eight, 38-22-36 wipeout fox counted nearly a half "C" note in tips. After bar cleanup duties, she stepped out into the late August chill of the deserted street. Her wind-flogged, shoulder-length mane coruscated beneath a street lamp like indigo neon. She scarved her hair and belted her red suede coat and appeared ten years younger than her thirty-four years. She stood on the sidewalk for a long moment, engorging her lungs, unloading tension with foggy air before she whipped her red-booted, centerfold-shapely gams toward her scarlet Mercedes parked down the street from the bar.

A simian-faced drug dealer monikered Tar Baby, aglow in pink leather, lunged from the black maw of an alley mouth to block her way.

She halted. "Tar Baby, you just did an uncool graveyard thing. What do you want?" she said icily as she darted her hand into her coat pocket to grip a .32 automatic.

His tiny dark eyes sparkled ravenously as he held out a thick bundle of "C" notes bound by a diamond- and ruby-studded money clip.

"The same thing I been wantin', sugar cunt, since I hit town last month. You! And to prove I ain't jivin', peel off a chunk of this bread and cop the greatest head on the planet," he crooned breathlessly.

"No sale. Get out of my way," she said in a cold, deadly voice. She remembered the pair of white would-be rapists she had ventilated into an intensive care ward six months before at this very alley after the bar closed. She hoped she would not be forced to repeat the bloody scenario as she said harshly, "Tar Baby, don't force me to harm you. Get out of my face!"

The giant threw back his glittery processed head and laughed. "I ain't gonna do that. I just decided I'm gonna kidnap ya fine ass and put ya in my bed this mornin'. Bitch, I'm claimin' ya for my woman!" he declared as he oozed toward her.

She snaked out the automatic and leveled it at his belly. "I'll burn you, Tar Baby!" she warned.

He studied her with hooded eyes for a moment before he took another step toward her. She stepped back, fired two rapid shots that chipped concrete at his feet, then she took aim at his head.

"Easy now, bad mama. You done won this round," he gasped with a horrific grin as he threw up his hands and backed into the alley toward his pink bubble top Eldorado in the alley.

"Nigger, next time you try to gorilla me, I won't miss!" she shouted as she pursued to the alley mouth.

She watched him squeal the Caddie away before she went to her car. As she drove through the sleazed Fillmore District, pangs of sorrow and guilt compelled fresh tears. "I should have checked on Toni in L.A. I should have tried harder to persuade her not to leave home," she told herself. "I helped to destroy her!"

She drove into a funeral home parking lot, deserted except for a hearse, and sat gazing at the fog-shrouded building, smoking a cigarette, preparing herself for the misery and pain awaiting. She noticed a driver in his cab parked at the curb. I guess Cass decided to take an earlier flight from L.A., she thought.

She left the car and climbed the stone steps of the mortuary. Her knees quivered as she opened the front door and stepped into the cathedral's quiet foyer. She exchanged nods with a drowsy old man behind a desk as she went down a blue-lit hallway to a shadow-haunted viewing room. There she paused on the threshold and watched for a moment the sleek, white leather-suited Cassandra Jones, model-singer-actress and family friend. Dionne Warwick look-alike, Cassandra sobbed as she stood beside Toni's blossom-banked casket, vivid in a spot of rose light. Lela went to Cassandra's side and kissed her cheek. They embraced as they gazed down at the shriveled ruin of Toni's corpse. The once-lush café au lait face had been blackened and sucked cadaverous by vampire heroin.

Lela groaned. "How, why has this happened to my baby? She was so pretty, so talented. Oh, I wish I could've found out who destroyed her and dumped her in that alley when I claimed her body! I would have blown his brains out!"

Cassandra said softly, "Lela, I knew who was responsible when you were in L.A."

"What!" Lela exclaimed.

Cassandra nodded her head, averting her eyes. "Yes, I knew. He pads in the penthouse in my hotel. I didn't tell you because I know you. I knew you'd kill him and get into trouble. So, I tipped off the cops instead. Horace Jenkins aka King Tut was busted early this morning with enough dope to bury him in the joint until he's an old man. I brought the L.A. Times to show you the story. Forgive me, Lela?"

Lela dropped her arm from Cassandra's waist and stared meanly into Cassandra's eyes. "I'll forgive you that. You called to tell me Toni was in the morgue, but why didn't you call me to tip me she was a pimp's slave and a junkie? Why, Cassandra? Why!?" Lela whispered savagely. "I could have brought her home and saved her."

Cassandra averted her eyes, lips atremble. Then she raised her stricken eyes, radiant with pain in her satiny tan face as she stagewhispered shakily, "Lela, I wanted to let you know about her when Tut opened her nose and turned her out . . . but Toni begged me not to. She was so miserable! So pitiful! Swore she could kick Tut and dope if I gave her a chance. She wanted to come back home to you clean. She told me that the night she OD'd. The night Tut dumped her in that alley. Lela, please try to understand why I didn't call you about Toni while she was alive." Cassandra broke into wild sobbing.

Lela said, "Forgive me, baby. I understand. Let's go home to stay forever, if you wish."

Cassandra blotted tears with a tissue and exclaimed, "Fantastic! I don't have to go back to L.A. until week after next to open a gig."

Lela kissed her cheek. "That's great, darling! I need you, and I've got a slew of outfits that will fit you." Lela put her arm around her waist and led her to the street.

Cassandra paid the waiting cabby, and got her overnight case before they drove away in the Mercedes. They exchanged sad, knowing glances as they passed a blistered, fire-gutted storefront with an askew smoke-blackened sign on its facade. LESEUR'S CLEANERS AND DYERS. Lela's hands shook on the steering wheel to remember how Lily, her mother, and Marcus, her husband, had been shot dead by arsonist bandits two years before at closing time. She heaved an anguished sigh as she recalled how her stalwart father, Benny, had become a pathetic alcoholic after the tragedy.

Moments later, Lela parked in front of the beige stucco house, in the heart of the ghetto, where she began her life. They strolled down the walk toward the front door. A fetal-ball wino slumbered on a sun-bleached wicker chaise that gleamed starkly in the blue wash of full moon. The chaise was ringed by a glitter-litter of empty shortdog bottles.

Lela went to his side. "Freddie, wake up!" she said as she gently shook him and slapped his spittled cheek.

He grunted and slumbered on.

She pulled his greasy topcoat up over his withered shoulders and looked down at the snoring derelict for a long moment, remembering how he and other close cronies of her father, their dreams deferred and clobbered, had once squabbled drunkenly on the wicker lounge over checkers, baseball, and politics.

She was tinged with pain as she remembered the summer day, the year before, when she found her father, a suicide, sprawled on the wicker lounge. "Damn! Will the Leseur jinx never end?" she asked herself with a shudder as she turned away to join Cassandra on the walk.

Lela glanced back at the grizzled septuagenarian. "I fixed the old angel a cozy place in the attic, but I guess he's a pneumonia buff."

They laughed feebly, then keyed in and entered the living room of the old house. Lela eye-swept her mother's dust-mantled vintage furniture she sentimentally had refused to replace, and the carpet cluttered with her teenage son's record player and albums. A faded poster of her idol, Huey Newton, on a thronelike chair, graced the wall over the fireplace.

"Excuse this joint, Cass," she said as she removed her coat and took Cassandra's.

Lela's face hardened as she sniffed the reefer-reeked air.

"Excuse me, Cass!" she said as she dropped the coats on a sofa, then stomped toward Marcus Junior's bedroom at the rear of the house.

Cassandra dropped her bag to the carpet. She let herself down on a sofa and lit a cigarette.

Lela froze at Marcus's bedroom off the kitchen when the corner of her eye snared the flash of a streaking white housecoat in the backyard. She glared through a kitchen window at Amazon Pat Williams, a sexpot twenty-five-year-old welfare divorcée mother of twin girls as she disappeared into her next-door backyard. Out of control with fury, Lela snatched up a rolling pin and charged out the kitchen door into the backyard. She stormed to the locked screen door of Pat's service porch and battered it with the rolling pin.

"Pat!" she hollered. "Pat! You rotten bitch! I want to pick a bone with you!"

She danced a frantic rigadoon of rage in the boiling silence of nonresponse for several moments before she smashed a gaping hole in the screen with the rolling pin. Quickly she reached in and unlocked the door, stepping into the service porch. Then she violently rattled the doorknob of the locked kitchen door, bashing the wooden club repeatedly against the door until Pat opened it, on chain.

Pat's sable eyes were electric with excitement and fear in her dollish yellow face, framed by a mass of disheveled, inky hair. The frightened eyes of her thigh-tall twins stared up at Lela through the aperture.

"Pat, I'm going to harm you the next time you violate Marcus and my house! Don't rap with him. Don't even look at him again. I dare you, bitch!"

"Lela, I'm not guilty, and I'm going to call the police if you don't split—now!" Pat warned as she slammed the door shut.

Lela went to a kitchen window and eye-locked Pat shakily dialing a wall phone. Lela's impulse to shatter the window with the rolling pin was squelched by the piteous faces of the squalling little girls.

Instead, Lela shouted through the glass, "Slut, call the police so I can get you busted for carnal knowledge of, and smoking dope with, a minor!"

Pat faltered, replaced the receiver, and left the kitchen with her twins in tow.

Lela gave up and went home, hurling the rolling pin into the sink as she went to stand in the doorway of Marcus's bedroom, trembling with rage. She stared at breeze-billowed curtains at an open window. Pat's escape route was confirmed by a red slipper on the carpet below the window. Lela trod her way through an assortment of hundreds of pounds of dumbbells and barbells. She went to the side of the bed and stared down at his six-four frame and head completely swathed in covers. His spurious snoring issued to hype up her rage. She leaned to whistle a thick leather belt from his jeans draped across a chair at the head of the bed. Then she yanked the covers off his nude body.

He stirred on his stomach, and she whacked his buttocks with the belt. He yelped and instantly rolled away to his feet on the other side of the bed.

"What's happening, Mama!?" he bellowed in a surprisingly deep baritone voice for a seventeen-year-old.

She gazed, sloe-eyed, at his nude splendor. His Apollo body, his voice, the long dangle of his hammer-headed womb sweeper reminded her of his late father. She was panged, swooned by erotic déjà vu remembering how Marcus Senior had orgasmed her into near convulsions of ecstasy in this very bedroom when her folks were away.

Junior's Ken Norton quality biceps writhed like milk chocolate pythons as he flung out his long arms toward her. The upturned palms of his gigantic hands jiggled melodramatic, confused innocence that infuriated her, galvanized her to knee herself across the bed. Her face was demonic as she pursued him about the room. He tripped, fell on his knees, trapped in a corner, covering his face with his arms and hands.

"You won't cut that worn-out slut loose, will you?" she screeched over and over again as she welted his back and buttocks with savage slashes of the belt until she stank of emotion sweat and her whip arm spasmed, cramped with fatigue, and dropped limply to her side.

Dry sobs humped his back as she released the belt to the carpet and staggered from the room into the kitchen. Cassandra put an arm around her shoulders.

Lela muttered, "I'm going to run through the shower. Please make some coffee."

Thirty minutes later, recovered Lela and Cassandra sat smoking and sipping coffee in housecoats at a breakfast nook table. Cassandra opened the L.A. Times to the drug bust story on King Tut, Toni's pimp destroyer, then passed the paper to Lela.

At that instant, Marcus, in a white terry cloth robe, opened his bedroom door. "Hi, Cass!" he said with a snowy-toothed smile.

"Hi, baby," Cassandra replied.

He came to embrace Lela from behind, leaned, and whispered into her ear, "Mama, I'm sorry I upset you. Pat's got my nose open. But I'm gonna cut her loose for you. No jive."

Lela turned her head to kiss his lips. "That makes me happy, and I'm sorry, too, darling, that I lost my temper. Angel, please don't disappoint Mama again. I love you!"

"Me you too, Mama," he said as he went to embrace and kiss Cassandra's cheek.

Lela said, "Baby, dear, shower off that slu . . . uh, woman's sti . . . uh, odor. I'll put some lanolin on your back before I go to bed."

"A'ight, Mama," he said as he left for the bathroom.

Lela read the L.A. Times's account of King Tut's drug bust. He was stopped by a uniformed squadron of officers when his chauffeur, Al "Skeeter" Lewis, ran a red light. Their nervous over-response to the relatively minor moving violation prompted them to search his gold Rolls after citation and a "no warrant, no want" radio checkout. They were taken into custody when three kilos of heroin were found in the Rolls' trunk.

Ironically, LAPD narcotics detectives had already focused on Tut on the basis of an apparently credible anonymous phone tipster (Cassandra). They had, just an hour before Tut's arrest, secured a search warrant for his hotel penthouse. They would have made the bust had not the traffic fluke occurred. Tut was now at liberty on a hundred thousand dollar bond on just drug charges. There was no evidence to support the allegation of the phone tipster that Tut was responsible for the OD death of Toni Leseur.

Lela had a genuine smile on her face for the first time since Cassandra notified her of Toni's death as she put the paper aside.

"Oh, Cass! Now I feel so much better about Toni. Too bad that snake isn't going to the gas chamber. But, he's a cinch to rot in the joint caught dead-bang with all that smack. Here's hoping he gets fifty years and then cancer from head to feet, if he survives the bit." Lela chortled as they banged coffee cups together and toasted Tut's ruin.

Marcus entered the kitchen and moved on into his bedroom.

Then, a paranoid notion suddenly seized Lela. She remembered the fierce rivalry that started between Cassandra's foster mother upon the car crash deaths of Cassandra's father, Sid, and mother, Carla, who had been Lela's best friend from childhood.

Lela stared across the table and thought of Cassandra's sulky anguish when later, on several occasions, the choicest boys gravitated to prettier, sexier Toni. Could Cassandra have harbored conscious or unconscious hatred through the years for Toni in sufficient volume to have played a role in Toni's ruin and death, Lela reluctantly asked herself.

Lela broke the heavy silence with a question. "Cass, since you live in that Tut bastard's hotel, I assume that you knew him, uh, at least by reputation before Toni met him?"

A transient frown flickered across Cassandra's face, not from secret guilt, or the question's content, but rather from a barely perceptible raw edge in Lela's voice and her piercing stare. "Why, yes, Lela, I met him first at a party he threw that first month I went to Hollywood and moved into his hotel. Why?"

Lela gnawed her bottom lip thoughtfully. "Cass, when you and Toni started dating, I spent a lot of energy cautioning you both about bullshit fast types . . ."

"That's the truth, Lela," Cassandra said with narrowed eyes.

Lela paused to light a cigarette, then violently exhaled a gust of smoke and shrugged her shoulders in dramatic confusion. "Then, why, pet, did you accept an invitation to a pimp's party? Huh?"

Cassandra's mouth twitched. "Look, Lela, I don't know where you're coming from with this quiz. But, I'm going to run down for you some realities of the 'now' Hollywood and how I wound up as Tut's guest without getting hip he was a pimp until he hit on me that night of the party. Tut fronts as a theatrical agent, has a boss suite in a Sunset Boulevard high rise with a receptionist-secretary. The whole flash bit. Even if I were a blue-eyed Farrah Fawcett type, the rat race to hit big is crowded and tough. Lela, you can't imag—"

Lela waved a hand to cut her off and said, "I took a brief flyer in Hollywood as an actress, remember? I scored for two-bit parts in two 'B' movies in a year and a half before I woke up and settled down with a husband."

Cassandra nodded. "Yes, I know, but that was years ago and rough, I know. But, Lela, Hollywood was when I met Tut, and is now absolutely infested with pretty faces and bodies of every conceivable color and type. All of them clawing for and fantasizing about that big golden dream shot into movies, commercials, or even permanent booking into some Jewish fat cat's bed in Malibu. Would you believe my rent and groceries backup while I struggled and dreamed happened to be a one-eyed black runt mechanic in Watts with filthy fingernails and banty legs?"

Lela shrugged, "I can believe that the shade of a straw can be a blessing when you're stranded in the Mojave Desert in July."

They laughed stingily. Lela scanned Cassandra's face as she flicked lighter flame to her cigarette.

Cassandra said, "Thanks, darling." She exhaled. "I went to Tut's party that night because I needed an agent like a wounded hemophiliac needs blood. And, darling, I was wounded by frustration. And as I said, Tut had that con front. Oh, I pulled Toni's coat that he was a fake that first week she left you and moved in with me."

Lela nodded. "I can dig how you met him. Now, tell me how he shot down intelligent Toni and became her boss right under your hip nose. Huh?" Lela pressed with cold sarcasm.

Aggravation hardened Cassandra's face. "Lela, Toni was broke. I was broke. We were running on the rim. I wasn't in L.A. when he shot her down. Toni and I, like nearly everybody else in tinsel town, snorted a taste of coke. In our case, when it was laid out freebie by the host or hostess of parties we attended to make the right contacts.

"Toni was wild about the dust! Well, anyway, while I was away doing a singing gig in Cincy, Tut cut into her and jammed her nose with some pure crystal coke. Then he flashed his monstrous bankroll for her, all in thousand dollar bills. Then he shoved a wad of them into her bosom to keep. Temporarily. She went to his bed. He conned her that he had fallen in love and she was so beautiful that he wanted her as the nonworking queen of his stable.

"He stashed her in a suite below the penthouse, and for a month he kept his promise while he kept her nose dirty with coke laced heavy with pure 'H'. Horse, not Tut, turned her out and became her real boss. She was scratching and nodding and flipping car tricks at Sunset and La Brea when I got back to L.A. two months later.

"She was visiting me in my pad her last night after her street gig. Tut called down to tell her that a shipment of dynamite smack had just come in. She split to the penthouse excited as hell. The next time I saw her was in the morgue after the L.A. Sentinel carried a description of a black girl found in a Watts alley OD'd. I was certain I'd find Toni there from the paper's description of that tattoo of a blue swan on her left wrist. Now, Lela, may I get out of the dock?"

Lela said, "All right, after you tell me how you became the greatest psychic there ever was."

"What!" Cassandra exclaimed. "One of us needs help, Lela. And it ain't me."

"Nor me, Cass. Just tell me how you could know all of the fine details of how that dirty nigger trapped my baby," Lela intoned.

Cassandra heaved a sigh of exasperation, stood, and leaned in to eye-lock Lela. "You just read about 'Skeeter' Lewis. He's Tut's chauffeur and around-the-clock flunky. He told me! We're tight, and secretly, he hates Tut. Satisfied, Lela? Now hear this! Toni was a finer fox than me, and it gave me lots of pain boo-koo times. I envied her. Goddamn, I envied her! But I loved her like a blood sister, Lela. I would have died for her! Can you believe that, Lela?"

Lela averted her eyes, stood, and whispered against Cassandra's cheek as she embraced her. "Yes, baby, I know you loved Toni. I'm sorry. Will you forgive me?"

Cassandra dinged to her and smiled. "Why not, play mama?"

They disengaged. Lela went to the threshold of Marcus's bedroom door, eased it open, and eye-signaled Cassandra to her side. They peered at Marcus fast asleep on the bed in his robe with a beatific smile on his delicately sculpted lips.

Lela whispered, "Cass, isn't he his father's double?"

Cassandra nodded and smiled. "He's a heart stomper, all right."

"I don't think I'll awaken him to lanolin his back. Cass, after losing Mama, Papa, my sweet hubby, and Toni, if anything happened to him . . . !" Lela paused to squeeze Cassandra's arm until she winced. "I'll cash in my chips. I just can't take another death blow!" Lela continued in a deadly serious voice as she closed the door and they turned away.

They went to collect Cassandra's bag and coat in the living room, then embraced each other's waists as they walked up the staircase leading to upstairs bedrooms to get a few hours' sleep before Toni's funeral in the morning.

Embattled ex-Watts resident Horace Jenkins, now notorious from coast to coast as King Tut, paced his penthouse terrace in Hollywood beset by maximal tension. He was inspired to his duck-to-water hijack of the provocative moniker by one of the three mud-kickers in his painfully modest stable. Lured by the street bell ring of the moniker, seven choice white girls swooned into his stable. This shortly after the perceptive mud-kicker had been electrified by his startling resemblance to a magazine picture of the mummified monarch's death mask.

Jenkins's self-coronation occurred in the mega-explosion of media hype, in the big-buck huckstering of replicas of the ancient Egyptian boy king, of ersatz gold reproductions of statuary and artifacts looted from his centuries-endusted tomb by archaeologists under the guise of their grave-burgling science.

Street Pharaoh Tut halted his pacing of the terrace to stare across

a midnight ocean of Hollywood neon at a pair of distant police heli-
copters attacking the bleak enclave of Watts with spy lasers of fiery
light. He shaped a triumphant smile in the throes of cerebral mas-
turbation. He ecstatically mulls the no-price odds that he, a mulatto
trick baby spewed out on the toilet floor of a Watts bucket of blood
saloon from the womb of his white whore mother, would survive to
become a superstar player, Rex of Hollywood's Kingdom of Vice.

Suddenly his rapture clabbered. He remembered his drug case
on the court calendar impending that could depose him to a prison
cell. He reminded himself that from a hundred gees, his bankroll
had shrunk to a paltry two grand. And that his weekly nut for stable
logistics and his own support and hedonistic fulfillment was close to
five grand.

His chest inflated with tension again. He paced once more,
with his recently gem-burdened, now mouthpiece-denuded, hands
jammed into his gold silk-brocaded robe pockets. For the thou-
sandth time he cursed the Hillside Strangler and the heat his murders had generated in Hollywood. The glut of strangler task force
cops on the streets, and the special hooker task force of undercover
and uniformed cops walking and riding had compelled him to ship
all but one of his ten-girl stable to bordellos in several states. The
thought that madams skimmed fifty percent off each of his girls'
earnings roiled his entrails with irritation.

He sat down on a gold satin chaise beside an aquarium stocked
with butcher piranha fish for a blow of coke. He snorted dust from
his diamond-encrusted spoon strung on a gold chain around his
neck. Then he took a hamster from a cage beside the tank and
grinned as he watched the butcher fish churn the water to bloody
froth as they slashed and tore the rodent to pieces and devoured it.

He saw the reflection of Skeeter, his chauffeur and long-term
flunky, in a mirrored panel of the tank coming toward him. He
had a worried expression on his once-handsome, lye-scarred face,
inflicted by one of his girls ten years before when he was the Big

Apple's top player. Suspecting the reason for Skeeter's approach, Tut stiffened and glared at Skeeter's reflection as he reached him.

"Say, man, I got bad news. Joy is sick. Like I told you, she needs a doctor, bad! She's got terrible pains in her side. She's pouring sweat." Skeeter toyed with the lapels of his blue Petrocelli sharkskin suit.

"Put that ho on her flight to Nevada, nigger. I promised Kate the bitch would be there on time. I ain't gonna let that fulla-shit-bitch foul my word. 'Sides, ain't no ho nineteen with her asshole pointing to the clay can be too sick to work in my game book," Tut growled as he evil-eyed his man's reflection in the tank mirror.

Skeeter shrugged. "The ho is going to collapse at Kate's the first trick she turns if she don't on the plane. She's too sick to dress. But, it's your ho, my man," he said as he turned and walked away.

"Dress that ho, Skeeter, and ship the bitch!" Tut shouted to his back.

Skeeter halted at the entrance to the sunken living room, then turned in slow motion fury to stand glaring at Tut's reflected face. The jaws of his monster face quivered anger and empathy for Joy, whom he secretly adored.

"Cocksucker! I'm going to ice you one of these days!" Skeeter screamed to himself. "All right," he managed to say blandly as he turned and disappeared into the living room.

After several blows of cocaine, twenty minutes later, Tut left the terrace. He traveled across the dazzling expanse of the lavender and gold-motifed living room toward a line of bedrooms, passing Skeeter's half-open bedroom door on his way to Joy's room.

"Hey, man," he heard Skeeter say behind him.

He went back to face him in the hall outside his room. "Yeah, what is it?" Tut said irritably.

"Save yourself a trip to Joy's room. She'll never make the plane to Kate's."

"What!?" Tut exclaimed.

"Your ho is dead, man," Skeeter said in a shaky whisper as he turned away into his bedroom with fists knotted and trembling at his sides.

Tut hurried down the hall to Joy's open door and recoiled aghast, staring at the perfectly formed wee chocolate doll lying nude on her back with an odious green slime oozing from between her legs. Tut retched as he galloped back to Skeeter's open door.

"What happened to the ho, nigger?" he shouted.

"Her appendix busted. My mama went that way," Skeeter whispered as he sat on the side of his bed and wrung his hands.

"Nigger, you gotta take that dead bitch outta here and dump her!" Tut ordered.

"We could've saved her . . . if you hadda let me take her to a doctor like I begged you. I ain't gonna dump her in no alley like Toni. I'll get in the wind!"

Tut sneered. "Nigger, you ain't gonna split heaven for a dead ho. You copping two bills a week and freebie skag to shoot. Plus all the freebie cunt you can eat. And who but me would plan to spring for ten grand in the near future to make you pretty again? Nigger, dump the ho!"

"Please don't make me do that! She's dead legit. Ain't no need to dump her. I'll call in a city ambulance for a bad sick girl and let 'em find her dead. Won't be no hassle for you that way." Skeeter pleaded with his eyes locked on the carpet, certain that he would tip off his raging hatred if he looked at Tut.

"Sucker, I ain't investing no bread to bury no dead ho. Dump that stiff!" Tut hollered.

"I'll spring to bury her. I'll tell 'em she's my kid," Skeeter said as he picked up the phone receiver from a bedside table.

"Chump, that's mellow with me," Tut answered as he turned away.

Skeeter dialed, tears bursting as he fixed a homicidal stare on Tut's back as he stepped into the hall and pranced away.

Two weeks later, Lela, with Cassandra, stomped her Mercedes stallions toward L.A. to kill Tut for Toni's death after his lawyer had beaten his drug rap on the technicality of "illegal search and seizure." They had successfully contended that there was no reasonable legal justification for the squadron of cops to search Tut's machine after a petty traffic violation.

Eight hours later, Lela, disguised as a wrinkled, silver-haired senior citizen, sat in her two bills a day presidential suite in Tut's hotel. She had plotted in meticulous detail Tut's death with Skeeter and Cassandra. Moments later, the pair left Lela to set the death plot in motion.

Skeeter went to the penthouse, dropping down beside Tut seated on a sofa in the living room about to dial a phone. "Man, that call can wait!" he exclaimed with grifter excitement illuminating his ruined face.

"What happened?" Tut asked apprehensively as he replaced the receiver.

"Let's get out of here!" Skeeter said as he rose, darting a glance at a maid dusting furniture in a corner of the room.

Skeeter led him to the den, shutting the door. They dropped on a sofa.

"Remember Toni's roomie downstairs on the fifth floor?" Skeeter asked with bucked maroon eyes.

"Yeah, what about that square-ass zero bitch?" Tut said with a scornful hitch of his lavender silk-robed shoulders.

"You're playing her cheap, man. She ain't so square. I just rapped with her in the lobby. She begged me to connect her with some smooth, handsome player to take off a two hundred grand score from an old black broad in the presidential suite downstairs! I sure wish I didn't have this fucked-up face."

"You sure the bitch wasn't stoned?" Tut said as his grey eyes sparkled interest.

"Naw, man, she was sober as the born-again dude in D.C. Look, man, if you ain't interested, I'll cut New York Willie into the action and cop ten percent of the sting."

"Get on the horn and get that young bitch up here so I can quiz her."

Tut lifted the phone off an end table and put it in Skeeter's lap. He dialed the switchboard to ring Cassandra, now sharing Lela's suite. Within three minutes, Skeeter let her into the penthouse and escorted her into the den to sit beside Tut on the sofa, snorting coke up his straight, full-nostriled duplicate dead Pharaoh's nose. Skeeter started to sit down on the sofa, but he left the room when Tut glowered at him.

"Long time no see, pretty songbird. How you been?" Tut said as he brushed her cheek with his copy-sculpted, sensual-lipped Tut-ankhamun mouth.

"Like bad luck, in again, out again, Finnegan, gigging in boondocks clubs for a lousy bill or two and all the garbage I could eat."

Tut crooned, "Shit, ain't no reason for a boss fox like you to take punishment like that for slave change. I could pick up the phone and cop you a gig that would pay off two grand a week minimum if we could get an understanding."

Cassandra smiled. "Like I told you, Tut, when we first met, I just don't have what it takes to be a hooker."

At that instant, Lela walked out of the hotel manager's office with a receipt memoed briefcase, full of personal papers. The locked case left for the hotel safe was stuffed with newspapers.

In the penthouse, Tut leaned into Cassandra's face with his big, liquid, almond-shaped orbs wide in fake puzzlement. "Girl, why you so fucking square in this rich, fast, cold world where every motherfucker in it that's copping a big, easy, fast buck and silky living, ain't?"

She smiled ruefully, con lies. "You're mistaken about my squareness. I heisted a bank once with a dude I was hung up on, did a trey in the joint. I'll get down tough and caper if the payoff is in a class like the old lady with the long bread I told Skeeter about. Want me to give you a rundown on her?"

He slit-eyed her. "Yeah, Miss Willie Sutton, after you run down why you egged me, the greatest player on the planet, to hit on Skeeter to connect you with a player to take off Grandma what's-her-name?"

"Tut, I thought you were still salty with me because I got in the wind that night you hit on me to be your girl at your party. Okay?"

He nodded, "Go on, girl, run her down."

"Tut, the mark's name is Maggie Owens. She tipped me a 'C' note in a club to sing 'Embraceable You.' She went ape when I did. I was her houseguest until the end of my gig. I told her I was an orphan to hook her. Damn! She was uptight, all alone. She put her house up for sale and drove me to L.A. I can't get rid of her!

"She's the widow of a dude who was chief accountant for a big insurance company in Columbus, Ohio, before a stroke suddenly killed him. Then the company discovered that he had embezzled more than two hundred grand that they never recovered. She has it! I saw it! She'll be a cinch to take off it—"

Tut waved a hand through the air to interrupt her. "Whoa, Nellie! How long you know her?"

Cassandra thoughtfully chewed her bottom lip. "Oh, a couple months, give or take a day or two. Why?"

He shook his head. "Look, baby, you could be the most charming, adorable bitch there ever was. You could be so motherfucking sweet you shit Chanel Number Five turds. But, wouldn't no broad or stud young or old flash two hundred grand in stolen penitentiary bread and tip you to the rest of that private scam on no two-month foundation. She could be uptight as a saint in hell for a pal and she wouldn't tip to you. You gotta be fulla shit!"

She smiled indulgently. "I didn't say she tipped me to anything, Tut. I found out about her husband from newspaper clippings I found shaking down her house while she was at church. I saw the bread the night before we split for Columbus. I saw her, just before dawn from my bedroom window, digging in the yard of a vacant house next door. I peeped on her through the keyhole of her bedroom door when she took the bread from a plastic-wrapped strongbox and put it into a briefcase. Now, do you still think I'm bullshitting?"

He grinned sheepishly. "Naw, girl, Maggie could be a bird nest of gold on the clay, lying in the tall, sweet clover. Where is the bread now?"

She shook her head. "I don't know. That's why I need a player to play the bread out of her, wherever it is."

He slugged his knee with his fist. "Why don't you know where it is? Playing it out of her could take months. She ain't that kind of mark with all that bread in a briefcase."

She stared stupidly at him with mouth agape for a long bit before she mumbled, "It beats me where that bread is. I've been living in her suite since we got here four days ago. She hasn't been out of my sight except when I or she showered or used the john, and once when she went to the hotel beauty shop, empty-handed. I had dupes of her car trunk keys, and also of our suite key made at that key shop on the corner, which I guess was unnecessary, while she was in the beauty shop. That took less than ten minutes. I searched the suite immediately and the car trunk later in the morning while she was asleep." She fluttered her hands helplessly. "Tut, what do you think?"

He patted her knee. "You overlooked it in that big suite. She probably stashed it behind a loose ventilator cover . . . unless she stashed it somewhere in the undercarriage of her ride along the way to the coast while you were asleep. How long did you get to search the suite?"

"Not a helluva long time because she only got a hair trim."

"Well, you musta overlooked the stash. Give me the dupe to the suite and Skeeter and I will fine-tooth it while you lug her out to a restaurant or a show tonight. If we don't score in the suite, I'll have Skeeter crawl under her ride and search the undercarriage."

She obdurately shook her head. "No way, Tut. No unless we split fifty-fifty."

He shaped a cunning grin. "Sure, clever baby, that's cool."

She dug into her cleavage and handed him the dupe suite key.

"I'll take her to see *Close Encounters of the Third Kind* at eight. Okay?" she said as she stood. "Oh, I forgot a stop we made in the Big Bear area. For sentimental reasons, she wanted to see a cabin her husband once owned that she honeymooned in a zillion years ago."

Tut finger-stroked his chin. "Was she out of your sight up there?"

"Hell, yes, for an hour or so while she prowled several caves until she found the one where she said she and her husband had made love in almost fifty years ago. I had driven the last six hundred mile-leg of our trip into California, so I took a nap in the car. I was too pooped to have a flaming desire to see a cave where a dead dude had humped her before I was born. But, what's the diff? Like I told you, Tut, she brought that briefcase into the suite."

They shook hands to bind their deal, then he walked her to the penthouse private elevator. She pecked his cheek before stepping into the elevator, and he turned away with his face aglow with easy, big, fast-buck excitement.

At seven forty-five that evening, Lela placed the receipt for the dummy briefcase in the hotel safe faceup on a dresser top before she and Cassandra left for the movie. At eight fifteen, Tut and Skeeter used the dupe key to enter the target suite. They searched the suite, Lela's bags, even Cassandra's, and even beneath Lela's and Cassandra's clothes hanging in the walk-in closet. Every aperture of the suite was checked out with a flashlight.

After an hour and a half of reach-and-stoop sweaty labor, mostly Tut's, Tut panted, "Skeeter, that briefcase ain't in this suite."

Skeeter looked at pimp Tut dripping sweat and struggled mightily to keep a straight face as he said, "Naw, man, ain't no way it's here. Guess, like you said, if it ain't here, it's gotta be stashed somewhere underneath the old broad's ride."

Tut heaved a sigh. "Yeah, we'll check out the ride in the parking lot this morning. Let's get the fuck outta here for a blow of frost and a bath. I don't see how square chumps can hump eight hours a day on a gig."

Skeeter said, "Let's mop this sweat off our faces before we hit the hallway," moving toward a box of tissues on a dresser top next to the briefcase receipt.

An eight by ten framed likeness of Lela in her old crone disguise stared myopically through heavy bifocals at Skeeter from the dresser top.

"Well, I'll be John Wayne's bastard brother!" Skeeter exclaimed as he picked up the receipt, passing it to Tut with con flabbergast twisting his awful face.

"Personal papers, her grey ass. That old bitch is leery of Cassandra! She sneaked that bread into that fucking hotel safe!" Tut exclaimed as he carefully returned it to its original spot on the dresser top.

Skeeter drawled, "Well, player, guess you gonna have to hit the old bitch with your game to cop that bread. Right?"

Tut glared at Lela's picture, "Yeah, it's gonna thrill the piss outta me to play a bitch older than bedbugs."

Skeeter perversely gave him a jarring fist in the shoulder, goading, "Cheer up, player! Maybe you won't have to suck her pussy to take off the sting," as they eased out of the suite.

At midnight, Cassandra called Tut to whisper that she had discovered the receipt for the briefcase atop Maggie's lingerie when she mistakenly opened Maggie's dresser drawer instead of her own while dressing for the trip to the movie. She explained to Tut that she had placed the receipt on the dresser top just before leaving the suite with the hope that he would spot it before he made an unnecessary search for the briefcase. Before she hung up she told Tut she sneaked the receipt back into Maggie's drawer when they returned from the movie.

At nine in the morning, she called Tut to report that Maggie had reclaimed the briefcase after hearing a TV news report of how bandits in Seattle had invaded a hotel and cleaned out the guests' valuables from the vault after forcing the manager to open it at gunpoint.

Then, at ten thirty, she breathlessly called Tut to report that she was calling from a hardware store where freaked-out Maggie had sent her to purchase a strongbox, shovel, and heavy-gauge plastic.

Immediately after the call, Tut turned to Skeeter seated beside him on the living-room sofa. "This is it, Skeeter! Cannon-ass it down to that hardware store down the block and cop a shovel!"

Ten minutes later, Tut and Skeeter, blue-jeaned and booted, sat in the hotel parking lot in Tut's gold Rolls. Fifteen minutes later they watched Cassandra carrying a bulky package and a shovel with its scoop wrapped in brown paper, and stooped Lela, clutching a brief-case, enter her scarlet Mercedes. Chauffeur Skeeter tailed the Mercedes when Cassandra drove from the parking lot into sparse traffic.

Later, inside the Mercedes as Cassandra drove into the mountainous Big Bear area, Lela broke a long silence. "This used to be our favorite vacation spot when Marc was alive. It's beautiful, isn't it, Cass?"

"Very, Lela. Well, we are almost there where we . . ." Cassandra said as she glanced at the reflection of the Rolls in the rearview mirror, a half mile behind as she turned the Mercedes off the deserted highway to ascend a very steep mountain toward its heavily forested pinnacle.

"Yes, Cass, and now that we are only minutes away from doing it, I'm not thrilled a bit. In fact, in a way, I wish that fate had never put us in this position. I almost wish we didn't have to do it!" Then she heaved a heavy sigh and said bitterly, "But then, I remember my baby in that casket . . . and I know for her and the safety of other young women that monster must die!"

Minutes later inside the Rolls, several hundred yards from the mountaintop, Skeeter said, "They've stopped up there!"

Tut answered, "Yeah, to bury that bread. I was wrong about the old broad being leery of that young bitch."

Skeeter said, "The old lady must really have her nose wide open for Cassandra to take her along to deep-six a load of bread like that . . . unless the old broad is senile."

Before Skeeter could say it, Tut said, "Drive the ride into cover.

We'll have to hike it from here to eyeball the spot where they bury that bread."

Skeeter slowed the car as it approached a crooked sign that read Picnic Area. He pulled the Rolls, as Tut instructed, off the road onto a narrow dirt road. Driving through a thick stand of trees to a mossy clearing containing several oaken tables for picnickers, Skeeter U-turned the Rolls to face the main road visible a hundred yards away. They got out and moved through heavy brush toward the summit of the mountain, halting and staring at the gaping mouth of a cave fifty yards away.

A half hour later they peered through heavy brush at Lela and Cassandra leaving the cave empty-handed except for the shovel. A cabin sat a hundred yards above the cave.

That must be the cabin where the old broad honeymooned, Tut told himself. They watched as Cassandra pulled the Mercedes away down the road toward the flatlands.

"Let's go!" Tut exclaimed as he turned and led Skeeter back toward the Rolls.

As they reached the picnic clearing, Lela and Cassandra, armed with the shovel, stepped from the cover of thick brush at the clearing perimeter, several yards behind Tut. He whirled and recoiled in shock from Lela's mint image of Toni stripped of gray wig and heavy bifocals, leveling an automatic at his chest. At the same instant, Skeeter pulled a length of iron pipe from his boot.

"Yes, you dirty cocksucker, I'm Toni's mama!" Lela intoned with a hideous face as Tut turned to flee.

Skeeter smashed the pipe against the side of his head, and as Tut stumbled past Cassandra toward the brush, she chopped a long, deep gash into his throat with a violent swing of the shovel. Tut collapsed on his knees. As Lela went to stand over him she fired several rapid shots into the back of his head and Tut fell dead on his back.

The trio dragged him to the Rolls, put his corpse on the front seat. Then they got in with Skeeter behind the wheel, and he drove to park the Rolls and set the emergency brake near the inclined edge of a thousand foot cliff near the parked Mercedes. After they got out, Skeeter retrieved a five-gallon can of gasoline from the trunk of the Mercedes, saturating Tut's body and the Rolls's interior with the gasoline. He leaned in, released the emergency brake, and scampered away from the car.

As the death car rolled toward the abyss, Lela fired into the gas tank. The Rolls exploded in a ball of fire as it tumbled off the cliff. Then the trio hurried to the Mercedes, and Lela sprinted it away down the mountain toward the flatlands.

At that instant, bathrobed Marcus flipped breakfast pancakes in the Leseur kitchen, then sat down at the breakfast nook table to wolf down the flapjacks. Finished, he was about to rise when he froze, seeing Pat in a pink bikini moving through the unusually hot and humid sun-dazzled air toward the open kitchen door.

"Hey, baby, I just copped some dynamite smoke!" she said as she entered the kitchen. She slid her pulse-hammering curves against him at the table, extracting a fat joint from the satiny lair of her wipe-out breasts.

"Pat, you ain't got no business here," he said raggedly as she tongued his ear and darted her hand beneath his robe to finger-stroke his obese womb sweeper quickening to the perpendicular despite his sincere promise to Lela to cut Pat loose.

"I ain't gonna stay, baby. I just wanted to share this bad shit with you," she crooned as she lit the bomber with a lighter from her awesome valley of rut.

She drew deeply, with slumberous eyes, before she placed the angel dust brain-bomber between his lips. Then he drew on it deeply, and they passed the joint between them until it roached.

"Whew!" he blew as he stripped off his robe.

"Ain't it some bad shit, baby? It's spiked with angel dust," she slurred as she dropped her head to his naked lap, massaging her cheek against his crotch thicket.

"Don't know . . . This shit has got me on fire!" he gasped as he savagely jerked her head up by her hair to stare malevolently into her eyes.

"Baby, please don't look at me like that!" she bleated as she tore at his hand to free her hair.

He saw her face transpose hideously. Then he stood and lifted her by her hair to her feet as she shrieked in pain and raked bloody rills down his face with her fingernails. He hoisted her over his head and hurled her against the wall where she lay stunned in a sitting position, moaning.

He galloped nude from the kitchen through the house and out the front door into the quiet street, gabbling like a Holy Roller possessed by the Holy Ghost and the Divine Fire. He bowled over an elderly black man who had known him since birth when the man tried to block his way on the sidewalk in front of the Leseur house. Marcus raced to the crowded street of a business district a block away where he stopped to seize a parking meter. He bent it backward and forward to loosen it at its base before he wrenched it from its foundation.

Pedestrians screamed and scattered in his wake like sheep before a panther as he shattered shop windows with the parking meter for two blocks before a police car blocked his way at an intersection. He clubbed the cruiser windshield to smithereens before the pair of cops leaped to the street and leveled pistols on him.

"Put your hands over your head!" one of them commanded as they leveled their guns on him from behind the cruiser.

Marcus charged them with a snarl, and they emptied their guns into his head and chest. Lela's "I'll cash in my chips if anything happened to him . . ." child fell riddled, encrimsoned into the street. Dead.

*A preview of*

# MAMA BLACK WIDOW

# 1

# MAMA YOU MOTHER . . . !

She lay beside me in the late March night, naked and crying bitterly into her pillow. The bellow of a giant truck barreling down State Street in Chicago's far Southside almost drowned out her voice as she sobbed, "What's wrong with me, Otis? Why is it so hard for you to make love to me? Am I too fat? Do you love someone else? Yes, I guess that's it. And that's why you haven't married me. This is 1968. We've been sleeping together for a whole year. I wasn't brought up like that. Let's get married. Please make me Mrs. Tilson. I hope you're not stalling because I married twice before."

I just lay there squeezing the limp flesh between my sweaty thighs and feeling desperate helplessness and panic.

I danced my fingertips down her spine and whispered tenderly into her ear, "Dorcas, there's no one else. I think I've loved you since we were very young. I just have to stop drinking so much. Maybe we'll get married soon. Now, let's try it again."

She turned over slowly and lay on her back in a blue patch of moonlight. Her enormous black eyes were luminous in the strong ebony face. Desperately I set my imagination free and gazed at her tits, jerking like monstrous male organs in climax.

I felt an electric spark quicken my limpness. Frantically I closed my eyes and gnawed and sucked at the heaving humps. Her outcries of joyful pain pumped rigid readiness into me.

She pinched it. She moaned and held herself open.

She screamed, "Please! Please, fuck me before it falls again."

I lunged into her and seized her thighs to hold them back. But as I touched her fat softness I felt myself collapsing inside her.

I was terrified. So I thought about Mike and the crazy excitement I had felt long ago when I pressed my face against his hard hairy belly. Then in the magic of imagination, instead of Dorcas it was the beautiful heartbreaker Mike that I smashed into.

Later, I lay and watched Dorcas sleeping. Except for added weight and faint stress lines etched into the satin skin, she looked the same as she had on that enchanted spring day when I first met her twenty years before.

What a chump I had been then to dream that the daughter of a big shot mortician could really be mine.

Mama had warned me then, "Sweet Pea, a slum fellow like you don't have a chance with a girl like that. Her father will see to it. If anyone despises poor niggers more than white folks, it's high class niggers like him."

Mama had been right. He had helped to marry her off and broken my heart. The prejudiced bastard was dead now.

By sheer chance I had run into Dorcas a week after his death. She was a trained mortician, but she was lonely and needed help.

I knew right away that there was still lots of warm sweet voltage between us. Two days later I moved from Mama and the tenement flat where I had spent most of my life.

I hadn't dated a guy since I moved into the funeral home with her. I put off marrying her because I knew that freakish creature I called Sally was still alive inside me. I was afraid of Sally. I couldn't marry Dorcas until I was certain that the bitch Sally was dead.

I thought about the freshly embalmed corpse of Deacon Davis lying in the mortuary morgue downstairs. I would have to groom and dress it by mid-morning for viewing in the slumber room. I tried until dawn to sleep. But it was no use. I couldn't get the corpse of Deacon Davis off my mind. I decided to prepare the Deacon and get him off my mind.

I eased out of bed and slipped on a robe and slippers. I took a ring of keys from the dresser top and went down the front stairway to the street. I went down the sidewalk through the chilly dawn to the front door of the mortuary.

I unlocked the door and stepped into the dim reception room. I walked across the deep pile gold carpet into the office. I switched on a light and sat down at the old mahogany desk. I took a fresh fifth of gin from a drawer and sipped it half empty.

The shrill blast of the desk phone startled me. I picked up and said, "Reed's Funeral Home."

Mama's high pitched, rapid voice chattered over the wire, "Sweet Pea, it's been over a week since you visited or called me. You know I have a bad heart and I'm all alone. Don't let that woman make you neglect your Mama. Think about it and let your conscience be your judge."

Before I could reply, she hung up. I started to call her back, but decided against it. I took two more belts of gin and went through the darkened chapel on my way to the morgue at the rear of the building.

The heavy odor of spoiling flowers and the harsh chemical stench of preserved death burst from the slumber room. I walked into its shadowy blueness and paused beside a cheap chalky casket with a bouquet of stale blossoms laying on the foot of it. There was a poignant message scrawled on a smudgy card: "Happy journey, Papa, to the arms of sweet Jesus. See you soon. Lettie, your loving, lonesome wife."

I stared down at the tired dead face, creased hideous by the life-time terror and torture of its blackness. I remembered the puckered emblems of hate on the corpse's back.

I turned away from the pitiful corpse wrapped in the shabby suit. I walked unsteadily down the long murky hallway to the morgue.

I opened the raspy door. There he was, a skeletal black blob on the porcelain table that gleamed whitely in the half darkness.

I walked across the room and the scraping of my feet against the concrete floor was like shrieking in the tomb quiet. I flipped on the high intensity lamp over the table. I slipped on rubber gloves and stood hypnotized, sweeping my eyes up and down the white haired wasted corpse.

I shook with rage as scenes and sounds of the awful past shattered and filled the bright stillness. I was nine years old when the corpse everybody respectfully called Deacon Davis lived on the third floor of the Westside tenement where Mama still lives.

I remembered that first time in his apartment. His hand was hot between my legs, caressing the throbbing tip of my stiff little organ.

His voice was hoarse with excitement, "Kiss mine and lick it, you dear little boy, like I did to yours. Mine is a magic wand to make any wish come true when you make it cry tears of joy."

I put the long crooked thing in my mouth until I spat its slimy tears. I cheated the wand and made two wishes: That poor Papa found a steady job. And that Mama wouldn't be so bossy and cruel to Papa anymore.

To my complaints of wishes unfulfilled, the Deacon would grin and say, "I know what's wrong. My wand must cry deep in your hunger, my dear boy."

For more than a year, until he moved away, the Deacon shoved his wand deeply into me. The Deacon sure ruined me. He really did.

I leaned over the corpse and roughly jabbed my thumbs into the sunken eye sockets. I pushed back the withered eyelids and stared into the brown orbs filmy and vacant.

I whispered, "Dear Deacon Davis, you can't know how thrilled I am to see you again. I just don't want you to go to your grave unpunished. You bastard child-raping freak. I'm going to shave you and dress your nappy hair. Then I'm going to punish you for ruining me. But no one will know except you and me, dear Deacon Davis."

I groomed the corpse and got a razor-sharp scalpel. I lifted his wrinkled shaft and held it erect at its tip between a thumb and index finger. I stood there with the glittering blade in my hand.

I glanced at the Deacon's face. The blank sable eyes were staring at me. I felt suddenly queasy and faint. The scalpel clattered to the table top. I jerked my hand away from the shaft and pressed the eyelids down. I just couldn't do a vicious thing like that even to a filthy freak like Deacon Davis.

I was putting underwear on the corpse when it groaned as trapped air escaped its chest. I went to the office in a hurry for a stiff drink of gin. I came back to the morgue and split the burial suit coat and shirt down the back and dressed the body.

I wheeled the white satin-lined casket to the side of the table. I attached pulleys over the table to the corpse and lowered it into the casket. I wheeled it into the slumber room for viewing by mourners who believed the Deacon was holy.

Funeral services for Deacon Davis were held two days later. The anguished wails of his surviving brother and sister moved me not at all.

I drove the hearse to the cemetery. Two elegant black limousines driven by chauffeurs Dorcas hired at a ten dollar fee followed behind me. At least thirty private cars behind them crawled through the dazzling sunshine to the grave. The Deacon was well thought of all right. But then I'm sure that the mourners didn't know about his dirty passion for little boys.

A nice funeral like that was much more than the Deacon deserved. But I was really glad I hadn't used that scalpel on the Deacon. I've always, at least in one respect tried to be like my idol, Martin Luther King, Jr. To not hate anybody.

To tell the truth, I've never really hated a living human soul except cops. There may be cops who are human, but I've never known any.

The day after the Deacon's funeral I called Mama more than a dozen times. I didn't get an answer and the line was never busy. I was awfully worried, so that evening around seven I killed the fifth of gin and drove my old Plymouth to the Westside.

I drove past raucous clusters of ragged kids frolicking on the sidewalks and stoops in the twilight-down Homan Avenue past 1321, the six flat slum building that my idol and his group had taken over in February, 1966. The plan had been (in violation of the law) to collect the rents and spend the money to make the building fit for human occupancy.

I parked at the curb at the end of the block. A gorgeous black brute striding down the sidewalk toward me mesmerized me. The bulgy thigh muscles undulated against his tight white trousers. I forgot all my resolutions to keep Sally shackled and scrambled to the sidewalk and stood fumbling with my key ring.

His raw body odor spiced with the scent of shaving lotion floated deliriously on the warm air. I inhaled hungrily. I was flaming. I really was. He came abreast of me and I saw the imprint of his huge dick. I was dizzy with a hot roaring in my head. I almost fainted with excitement. I really did.

I had an insane urge to stroke his thing. Instead I caressed my eyes over his crotch and then waltzed them to the depths of his dreamy brown eyes, searching for a flicker of sweet kinship for "the" secret message. I saw only a cold quizzical indifference as he passed me. The beautiful bastard was straight!

Almost instantly I felt like shouting with joy and relief that he was, and that the bitch, Sally, had been denied. I went down the cracked walk toward the grimy familiar front of the six unit building that Mama now owned.

I glanced at Mama's front window on the first floor. I saw the curtains flutter above a red and white sign, "Madame Miracle—Come In—Get the Golden Touch Blessing—Win and Hold Money and Friends—Discover How To Punish Your Enemies —Ward Off Evil Spirits—Enslave Sweethearts-Wives—Husbands—I am blessed with infinite wisdom and power."

I went past several cursing pre-teeners shooting penny craps on the stoop. I opened the front door and stepped into the building's musty vestibule.

A bandy legged old man in faded blue under-shorts was piling his ancient pocket watch wallet and small change on the rumpled heap of his puke stained trousers and shirt laying on the floor.

I paused beside him. I heard the door open leading to the first floor hallway. A tall elderly woman with a fierce face was standing with arms folded across her chest glaring down at the muttering old man.

She screamed in a shrill voice, "Nigger, this ain't our apartment. This is the vestibule. You drunk sonuvabitch. Pick up your filthy rags and get your black simple ass upstairs before I knock the shit outta' you."

The old man blinked his sad eyes like a frightened puppy and mutely worked his thick lips. I felt a sharp pulsing of sorrow and anger looking at his eyes. They were whipped, hopeless, pitiful eyes, so much like poor Papa's before he crawled off to die.

I went up the short stone stairway past the husky hag and opened the splintered glassed door. I walked scabrous tile to Mama's door. I put my key in the lock and stepped inside. It was very dark except for cloudy rays of the street lamp that filtered through the living room curtains.

I said loudly, "Mama, it's Sweet Pea. Mama, are you here?"

There was no answer. I went down the hallway toward Mama's bedroom at the rear of the apartment. I thought about Mama's heart condition that was all in her mind. Her doctor had told me confidentially there was no organic trouble at all, just that Mama had deep mental needs for her attacks.

Then I remembered the movement of the curtains when I came up the front walk. I shivered. Mama had made enemies with her witchcraft. I wondered if she was dead and the murderer was still in the apartment. I stopped and stood uneasily at Mama's bedroom door, listening to the wild pumping of my heart.

I shouted, "Mama, are you here?"

No answer. The feeling was overpowering that something ghastly had happened to her. I almost knew somebody was behind that door. Perhaps the murderer was crimson with Mama's blood, panting, trapped, waiting for me with a butcher knife or hatchet in the dark in the other side of that door.

I decided to go back to the car. I turned and walked quickly back toward the front door. Then I glanced at the murky mirror on the wall next to the front door.

I froze. My legs wouldn't move any more. There was a kind of wavering shifting movement in the blackness behind me near Mama's bedroom. I almost tinkled on myself as I stared in the mirror and saw a mass of the blackness split off and glide toward me.

I spun around and faced the thing. I opened my mouth to scream, but nothing came out. The thing came closer and giggled. Then I saw a slash of white in a familiar black face. It was Mama in a long black robe smiling at me. I started crying in relief.

I blubbered, "Mama darling, why did you do that to me? Why didn't you answer when I called to you? OH! Mama, I thought something bad had happened to you."

Mama held her long arms open and crooned in her racing voice, "Come here and kiss me and tell me you love me. Mama didn't want to frighten her pretty baby, but I've been mad with you for neglecting me. Come on, Sweet Pea. Come to your Mama."

I felt a tremor of rage, not toward Mama really, but just for those spidery arms reaching out for me. In my anger I got the weirdest thoughts standing there. A lot like the terrible thoughts I used to get when I helped Mama with the dishes.

I'd have to lock my trembling hands together so I couldn't obey the terrifying impulse to stab a kitchen knife into her. It was awful because I love Mama and always will. But standing there in that hallway I thought how funny Mama would look without those arms. And what if I had found her not dead but with those clutching creatures chopped off cleanly with no pain, no blood, just open-mouthed surprise to see herself without them.

Then suddenly I was sorry for my mean thoughts. I rushed to her arms and buried my face in her bosom. She crushed me to her so hard I could hardly breathe. I raised my head and kissed her lips.

I sobbed, "Mama, I've missed you. I love you so much."

We stood there hugging and kissing like we hadn't seen each other in years. Mama led me into the living room and switched on a brass cherub lamp on a table at the end of the white sofa.

We sat on it close together. Mama scanned my face with bright black eyes. They were tiny unblinking eyes that I could never look into for long. When she was upset or angry they seemed to glow balefully.

But her eyes were warm and kind when she gently placed her hand on my thigh and said softly, "Sweet Pea, I see you and I just can't understand how we could live apart for a whole year. How do we stand it, precious?"

I didn't answer. I looked at her thinking how she'd changed; she'd been good looking and shapely down South. She'd even lost her thick southern accent with hard study and desire.

I moved my thigh away and said, "Now Mama, please don't start. It's not like I'm living out of town. I'm never going to stop calling you and visiting you. Think back, Mama, and remember what happened to Frank, Carol and Bessie. It makes me want to bawl to think about them.

"Mama, I'm the only kid you got left. I'm forty years old and this is my big chance to stand on my own and be a man. Try to understand. Help me, Mama. Only you know what I've gone through."

The warmness deserted her eyes. A toil coarsened hand thoughtfully pulled at the tip of her wide flat nose. I sat there on the edge of the sofa, waiting for her to speak, afraid that I had said the wrong thing. I'd always tried very hard not to displease her. I suffered when I did.

Finally, she clasped her hands beneath her chin and murmured in an icy voice, "That stale slut is poisoning my baby's mind against me. That's what she's doing. She's trying to make you stop loving . . ."

I took Mama's hands and pressed them against my face and cried out, "NO! NO! Stop it, Mama. You're wrong about Dorcas. She's a sweet person. She really is. She wouldn't try anything like that. Visit us, Mama, or let her come to see you. You would find out that she's a good woman."

Mama jerked her hands away and spat out, "I wouldn't go to that deceiving bitch's funeral. Sweet Pea, you're the biggest fool on God's green earth to forget how she and her high falutin' father treated you like dirt and hurt your heart.

"Sweet Pea, it's bad enough that you're sleeping with that treacherous slut. But before you leave me I want you to promise me that you'll never marry her. I'm telling you, Sweet Pea, that woman is a snake waiting to destroy you. Now say it, baby. Say that you won't break my heart and marry her."

I felt like I was suffocating under Mama's pressure. I could hardly breathe. I was so ill and angry. I really was.

I stood up and said sharply, "Mama, please! Give me a break, will you? I can't promise you that. Dorcas has always loved me. Her father didn't break us up. I did, with stupidity. She never really loved the two guys she married.

"Mama, I think I love her. I'm going to marry her as soon as I get my mind together. So don't call her names. I love you but I'm not going to stay tied to your apron strings and play with myself until I'm a dried up old man. I'm sick in my head, Mama. With Dorcas I might get well. So give me a chance and stop putting pressure on me. I can't stand it."

Mama's face was a tight black mask. I leaned over and kissed her forehead. I turned and walked to the front door. I glanced over my shoulder. Mama was coming toward me with her eyes almost closed and an odd smile on her face. Her silk robe rustled like a centipede snagging on autumn leaves. I flinched when she took my face between her palms and stared into my eyes.

She crooned too sweetly. "Sweet Pea, you're trembling. I know you're sorry you hurt me. I forgive you. Now come to your senses and come home soon to stay. We'll be so happy."

I twisted my face away and opened the door.

I said, "Mama, you didn't want me to make love to guys, and you don't want me to have Dorcas. I'm human. I have to have somebody."

She smiled broadly and said, "Precious, Mama will make a bargain with you. Come back home and I won't mind who your friends are, just so you respect me and your home and don't wear women's clothes. Fair enough?"

I could feel tears filling my eyes. I shook my head slowly and said, "Mama, you're really something, aren't you? You never give up. Respect? You don't give a damn about my self-respect. You wouldn't care if I went down on every guy in Chicago, just so I don't marry Dorcas. Right?"

Mama came toward me with those awful arms outstretched. I backed into the corridor and turned and walked toward the vestibule door.

I could hear Mama pleading, "Sweet Pea, don't leave like this. Come back and kiss me. I'm your Mama. I'm the only one who loves you. Please come back and kiss me. You're killing me, Sweet Pea. I feel an attack coming. You better come back here. Come back, Sweet Pea."

I went through the vestibule to the sidewalk. I glanced back at Mama's window. She had her head wedged between the white curtains, and her glittery little eyes were glaring at me. The street lamp shone through the telephone wires and imprinted a spidery web against the curtains.

## CASH MONEY RECORDS PRESENTS

# CASH MONEY CONTENT

www.cashmoneycontent.com

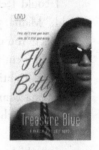

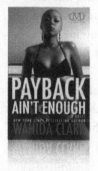

CASH MONEY CONTENT

CASH MONEY CONTENT

CASH MONEY BOOKS

CASH MONEY RECORDS PRESENTS

# CASH MONEY CONTENT

www.cashmoneycontent.com

CASH MONEY CONTENT

CASH MONEY CONTENT

CASH MONEY BOOKS